Milady in Love

G·K
Hall
&Cº

*Also by Marion Chesney
in Large Print:*

Tilly
The Marquis Takes a Bride
The Glitter and the Gold
My Dear Duchess
Sally
Lessons in Love
Silken Bonds
The Homecoming
The Romance
The Dreadful Debutante
A Marriage of Inconvenience
The Highland Countess
A Governess of Distinction
The Savage Marquess
The Scandalous Lady Wright

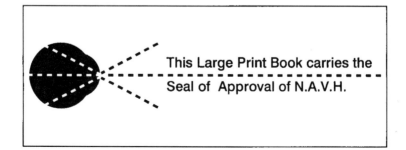

This Large Print Book carries the
Seal of Approval of N.A.V.H.

Milady in
Love

Marion Chesney

G.K. Hall & Co. • Waterville, Maine

Published in 2002 by arrangement with Lowenstein Associates, Inc.

G.K. Hall Large Print Core Series.

The text of this Large Print edition is unabridged.
Other aspects of the book may vary from the original edition.

Set in 16 pt. Plantin by Minnie B. Raven.

Printed in the United States on permanent paper.

Library of Congress Cataloging-in-Publication Data

Chesney, Marion.
    Milady in love / Marion Chesney.
      p. cm.
    ISBN 0-7838-9613-1 (lg. print : hc : alk. paper)
    1. Large type books.   I. Title.
PR6053.H4535 M48 2002
  823′.914—dc21   2001039797

Milady in Love

Chapter One

Viscount Anselm was thirty-three years of age, handsome, and rich. He was unmarried. And yet no one who knew his recent past was at all surprised that he was still unwed.

Ten years earlier, because of his extraordinary beauty, he had been as much the talk of London as any reigning belle. His golden hair, his sweet smile, and his charm made him a prime favorite with the ladies, while his strong physique, his ability with a small sword, and his reputation as a first-class whip ensured him the admiration of the sporting fraternity.

Then his uncle Viscount Anselm died, leaving in his care a gaggle of misses in their teens: three daughters, two orphaned nieces, and two illegitimate daughters.

The late viscount had been a crusty widower. He had alienated the affections of every respectable female relative who might have stepped in to aid the new viscount in finding husbands for this brood of young ladies he had inherited along with the title and his uncle's vast fortune.

He could have married, of course, and let his wife take some of the burden from his shoulders. But the young misses, with their hair-raising escapades, their flirtations with unsuitable men, and their constant giggles, kept him so busy that by the time he had escorted the last of them to the altar, he was a changed man.

He distrusted and disliked all females under the age of forty. The cares of his estates along with the cares of chaperonage had added stern lines to his face, and his once sweet and generous mouth was now perpetually set in firm, uncompromising lines.

Weary of the hot drawing rooms of London and the mindless frivolities of Season after weary Season, he let his town house and retired to his country residence, Trewent Castle in Cornwall.

Trewent Castle had been a lazar house in the old days and then a state prison. It had amused the late viscount to take it as his country home and then do very little about decorating or modernizing it. It stood on the cliffs, overlooking the sea, a stark battlemented place built of yellow bricks and surrounded by high grim walls topped with iron spikes, which had been placed there originally to keep the prisoners from escaping.

The new viscount planned to settle down to a quiet bachelor existence.

And then, only that week, the blow had fallen. His uncle, he knew, had been wild and

8

courageous in his youth and along with a band of other young Englishmen had done much to rescue French aristocrats from the guillotine. It appeared the ever-grateful Comte de la Falaise had died in Lisbon and left his daughter to the care of Viscount Anselm, without stating which viscount. This girl, a seventeen-year-old named Yvonne, was barely out of the schoolroom.

The Portuguese lawyers said this Yvonne would be arriving at Falmouth at the end of the month. They took it for granted that the viscount would accept the guardianship without question.

He traveled to London to consult his own lawyers. The head of the firm, Mr. Venables, shook his hoary head. Lord Anselm was within his rights to send a letter to Portugal by the next packet, refusing the guardianship. If he decided to accept it, however, said Mr. Venables, then the best advice he could give was to find some governess or respectable female to take the whole business off his hands.

"Again?" demanded the viscount testily. What about all those other governesses and companions he had hired to look after the late viscount's brood? Two had fallen in love with him to the point of embarrassment, one had become pregnant by a footman, and the others were so weak and silly they had proved useless.

"You have been very unlucky, my lord," agreed Mr. Venables. "But I urge you to place an advertisement in the newspapers, asking for a lady of mature years and long experience. Besides, this is only *one* young lady. And brought up in Portugal! They are very strict there. There will be nothing of the hoyden about her. Advertise locally. You have perhaps a better chance of finding someone of more stable character in the country than in London," added Mr. Venables, who had a very low opinion of the city in which he conducted his highly successful practice.

Although he did not entertain much hope of finding any reasonable-minded woman in the length and breadth of Britain, the viscount placed the suggested advertisement.

To his amazement, on the very day the advertisement appeared, his butler told him that a lady had answered it and was waiting in the hall.

"Put her in the library," said the viscount with a sigh. "Send in wine and biscuits. I shall join her in a few minutes. What is her name?"

"A Miss Patricia Cottingham from Middle Dean."

"From Middle Dean? Do you know the family, Fairbairn?"

Fairbairn, who was as old and hoary as Mr. Venables, shook his head. "Can't say as I can bring them to mind, my lord."

The viscount made his way down the oaken staircase some ten minutes later.

He did not usually keep callers of any rank or description waiting, but then he was sure this

Miss Cottingham would prove to be another faded, genteel, long-nosed antidote.

What a gloomy place this is! he thought not for the first time as the chill and bleakness of his home struck him afresh.

It seemed as if he had never had any time to redecorate it, what with squiring young misses to balls and routs in London in the Season and taking them to fashionable spas and watering places out of it.

He walked into the library and looked in surprise at the lady who was waiting for him.

She was certainly not in the first flush of youth; he thought she might be only a couple of years younger than he was. But she was plainly and stylishly dressed in a simple gray gown covered with a blue pelisse. She had thick fair hair under a neat straw bonnet. Her face was a calm oval, and she had well-spaced clear blue eyes. Her figure was shapely, and she held herself with an air.

But it was not her looks that struck the viscount so forcibly. It was the calm expression in her eyes and the way she stood very still, waiting for him, without fluttering or fussing.

For her part, Miss Cottingham saw a very tall man with guinea-gold hair cut in a Brutus crop. He was not dressed in any of the current extremes of fashion. His clothes were suitable for the country. He wore fawn leather breeches and top boots. A black riding coat, beautifully tailored, set off his strong shoulders and broad chest to advantage. His eyes were very blue and framed with thick sooty lashes. His nose was high-bridged, and his chin was firm. His eyelids were very heavy, which gave a strangely sensual, brooding look to a face that was otherwise rather severe.

"Miss Cottingham?"

She curtsied. "My lord."

"Pray be seated. You came very promptly in answer to my advertisement. Are you in some lady's employ at present?"

"No, my lord. I was employed by a Mrs. Benham in Exeter. She died earlier this year, leaving me an excellent reference — I have it, along with a previous reference — and a small sum of money. It was a long time since I had enjoyed a holiday, and I was grateful for the respite her bequest allowed me. Now I am ready to work again."

All this was said in a calm, steady voice.

"Let us, then, take the post with Mrs. Benham. How many young misses were in your charge?"

"Five, my lord. I have the reference here."

"I shall look at it later. In the meantime, I would rather you described the nature of your employment to me."

"Very well, my lord. I was with the family three years. I instructed the younger girls in the use of the globes, Italian, needlework, and in playing the pianoforte, as well as writing and spelling. The two elder girls — twins — I

12

coached for their come-out: how to curtsy, hold a fan, make conversation, and dress in a genteel manner."

The butler came in with cakes and wine and set the tray on a low table.

"We shall help ourselves," said the viscount, dismissing him.

When he had poured Miss Cottingham a glass of wine and when she had refused the cake and biscuits, he leaned back in his chair and said, "Tell me about your family, Miss Cottingham. Are they from Middle Dean?"

"No, my lord. They are from Pendry in Norfolk. I came to Exeter in answer to Mrs. Benham's advertisement. On her death, I found myself lodgings in Middle Dean."

"And your parents?"

"Both of them are dead, my lord. My father was vicar of St. Edmund's in Pendry. On his death, Mama and I found he had left very little. We struggled along. When Mama died a year later, I decided to make my own way in the world."

A gloomy greenish light filtered through the leaded windows. A huge grandfather clock beat out the time in a corner, and the crackling fire began to hiss as rain pattered down the chimney.

Lord Anselm found himself touched by Miss Cottingham's story. She had stated the details in a matter-of-fact voice, but he thought she had had a hard time of it.

He came to a decision.

"The situation is this, Miss Cottingham. My ward, Yvonne de la Falaise, will be arriving at the end of the month from Portugal. I have never seen her. She is French and has been brought up in Lisbon. I do not know if she can even speak English.

"I want a sensible lady to educate her enough so that she may be presented in London during the Season when she becomes, I think, nineteen years of age. I have no time to busy myself personally with such matters. Your job would be, in effect, to take the weight of the guardianship from my shoulders."

"Certainly, my lord."

"Let me have your references — thank you — but I doubt I shall even trouble to read them. Character is what matters and not references.

"It may strike you as odd that I should come to a decision so quickly, but I confess this matter wearies me already, and I have not even seen the girl.

"I shall travel to Falmouth to meet her, and when she is safely back here, I shall send my carriage for you. It has begun to rain. You had better go home by carriage. Make sure the coachman takes note of your address. Now, as to the matter of your salary. May I suggest fifty pounds a year?"

"You are very generous, my lord."

"You have to be more than just a governess.

You must also be friend, companion, and substitute mother. Do I make myself clear?"

"Yes, my lord."

He tugged at the bellpull beside his chair and ordered his carriage to be brought around to the front of the castle.

While they were waiting, he chatted about local affairs, all the time watching her calm face and graceful figure with pleasure.

So impressed was he with Miss Cottingham that he escorted her to the door of the castle himself and waited until she had been driven off.

Then he turned to his butler. "You may tell all future callers the post of governess has been filled, Fairbairn."

The viscount smiled with satisfaction. If there was one sensible woman left in England, then he had found her. Now all he had to do was to meet the chit at Falmouth when the boat from Portugal arrived and turn her over to Miss Cottingham's capable hands.

"Those, milady," said Gustave Bouvet, servant to Yvonne de la Falaise, "are the white cliffs of England."

"Tien!" exclaimed the little figure wrapped in furs beside him. "Then their size has been much magnified by report. *Not* impressive. I know I am *not* going to like this country, Gustave. What is England? A country without sun, I have heard, with great fat Englishmen

15

eating the roast beef all day long. Pah!"

Gustave remained silent, but he felt depressed. The day was gray and cold. Already he missed the sunshine of Portugal. As Yvonne's father had slowly and steadily gambled away his fortune, his servants had left one by one, until there was only Gustave, old Gustave, who stayed without wages and who had now transferred all his crusty devotion from the comte to this little child-woman, who was his late master's daughter.

Yvonne spoke English very well, having had an English governess until two years before her father's death, when even that worthy lady had tendered her resignation, saying she would not work for nothing. Gustave knew only a few words.

So when they landed, it was Yvonne who had to battle with the vexatious ceremonies of the customs house, where surly men tried to exact double fees for their baggage.

"And where is this milord who is to be my guardian?" demanded Yvonne, emerging flushed and triumphant after warring successfully with a rapacious customs official.

A liveried footman appeared at her elbow and enunciated with difficulty, "Do I address Lady de la False?"

"Yes," said Yvonne impatiently, "if by 'False' you mean Falaise."

"I am to take you to the Three Tuns, where my lord, the Viscount Anselm, awaits you."

He led the way to where a carriage was waiting outside the customs house. Yvonne's trunks were strapped on the back and the carriage moved off.

She looked curiously out the window. She had heard much about the wealth and cleanliness of English towns. But Falmouth appeared to consist of one long, narrow, rather dirty street with mean-looking houses crouched on either side.

But the harbor was very fine and commanded by Pendennis Castle, now a black silhouette against the darkening sky.

After a very short journey, they stopped outside the Three Tuns. The footman said his lord had waited dinner until her arrival and was abovestairs in a private parlor.

She followed the footman up a narrow staircase and along a twisting corridor.

He threw open a door at the end and announced her.

Yvonne tripped lightly in. Gustave stood in the doorway, awaiting his mistress's orders.

Viscount Anselm rose to his feet at Yvonne's entrance. His heart sank at the sight of her. She was the epitome of everything he detested in the gentler sex. And her very appearance and manner spelled Trouble.

He had persuaded himself that this new charge would be a meek, convent-bred foreigner, crushed, he hoped, into suitable modesty by a stern and disciplined upbringing.

The frivolous little creature in front of him looked uncrushable.

Her skin was golden, and she had huge black eyes fringed with ridiculously long silky lashes.

She had shrugged back the heavy fur mantle from her shoulders to reveal a dainty gown of India jaconet muslin cut quite low at the neck and ending at the hem in three deep flounces. Her hat was of gold straw chip, wide-brimmed and tilted to one side of her head in a decidedly rakish manner to reveal a head of thick black glossy curls.

She was quite small in stature, and she promptly sat down on a chair at the head of the table and looked up at the viscount in open admiration.

"Well, my lord," were the first words he heard Yvonne utter, "this is much better than I thought. I expected a fat old Englishman."

"Is that your servant?" demanded Lord Anselm, looking over her head to where Gustave, sallow and lantern-jawed, stood by the door.

"My Gustave. Yes."

"I am surprised. I should have expected a female servant to accompany you."

"And so she would, had there been any left. Papa gambled so much, he had no money to pay anyone, and only dear Gustave stayed." She kissed the tips of her fingers to Gustave, whose nutcracker face relaxed slightly, which was the most he could ever achieve in the way of a smile.

The earl signaled to his footman. "Take Gustave below and show him to his quarters. Tell the landlord to serve dinner immediately."

When the door had closed behind them, he sat down at the table next to Yvonne. "You must be exhausted after your journey, my lady."

"You may call me Yvonne."

"Thank you. Yvonne."

"No, I am not exhausted," said the frivolous creature, untying the ribbons of her hat and taking it from her head. "But I am so hungry. *Ma foi!* The food on board ship was disgusting."

"Did you suffer from seasickness?"

"Please?"

"Mal de mer."

"Not I. When do we go home?"

"In the morning. Why are you not wearing mourning, Yvonne?"

"Papa did not like mourning. Women wear so much black in Portugal, he said he did not want me to go around like a crow as well, even after his death. He mentioned that fact in his will. I have some pretty gowns, no? I had them made by the *best* dressmaker in Lisbon, and when Papa could not pay her, I sold my pearls to settle the account. One must always pay one's dressmaker, *n'est-ce pas?*"

"I believe in settling all my debts promptly," said the viscount stiffly. "I suggest you do not talk until after we have eaten. I have the head-ache."

Yvonne gurgled with laughter. "Ah, I see, in England it is the *gentlemen* who have the head-ache. Is it that you have the vapors as well?"

"That is quite enough."

Yvonne began to eat, at first with a hearty appetite, but then she appeared to lose interest.

"I would have thought you would have been hungrier," said the viscount.

"I *was* hungry," said Yvonne, pushing her plate away. "But such disgusting food ruins the appetite. I cannot relish it. The meat is half raw, and the vegetables are not boiled enough to make them soft. This wine is miserable. How much a bottle?"

"Four shillings and sixpence."

"A *bottle?*"

"Yes."

"Robbery!" said Yvonne, much shocked.

"Did no one ever tell you it is very bad manners to criticize your host's table?"

"Of course. I should not dream of doing such a thing were it *your* table. But this is a common inn. *Very* common."

The viscount surveyed her with displeasure and irritation. She had not said one word of gratitude. Instead, she was going on in a very high-handed manner.

He gave a sigh. Thank goodness for Miss Cottingham.

Yvonne flashed him a look of quick sympathy.

"Ah, I *am* behaving badly, and you are wondering why you should be plagued with such a charge. I am irritable. I feel very *foreign*. But I am grateful to you, milord viscount. *Very*."

"I do not expect any show of gratitude, I assure you," he said stiffly.

"Oh, yes, you *do*. This cheese now is good, and the butter excellent. This abominable fare does not appear to affect your appetite. No doubt you were in the army."

"I was. But I am never overnice in my tastes when staying at, as you put it, a *common* inn."

"Then you should be," said Yvonne, raising delicate arched eyebrows. "How can they improve the cuisine if every guest is as stoic about it as you are yourself?"

"Yvonne, you force me to point out that I am your guardian, I am considerably older than you, and it would be more becoming if you showed a modicum of respect."

Yvonne spread her fingers in a Gallic gesture. "I am *all* respect, milord. You say you are considerably older than I. You wear well."

"Thank you." Her enormous black eyes were fixed on his face, and the viscount began to feel overwarm.

"I have employed a governess-companion for you," he said.

"A companion would be pleasant," said Yvonne, "but I am not in need of a governess."

"You being so well educated," mocked the viscount.

"Me being so well educated," agreed Yvonne placidly. "I speak English very well, French is my native tongue, and I also speak Spanish and Portuguese like a native."

"A facility in languages is admirable, but a lady must be cognizant with the gentler arts, such as . . . such as sewing, watercolor painting, playing the pianoforte, curtsying. . . ."

"I curtsy to perfection." Yvonne darted lightly from the table and sank into a court curtsy, looking up at him in a teasing way from under her lashes.

"Sit down!" he barked.

Yvonne gave a little shrug and resumed her place at the table.

The viscount summoned up his sternest tones. "We shall remain silent for the rest of the meal."

Yvonne bowed her head meekly over her plate. From the occasional shaking of her shoulders, he knew she was trying to stifle a fit of the giggles.

When the landlord and his maids came in to clear the dishes, the viscount hailed him with relief. Yvonne was ordered to bed and told that they would set out for Trewent Castle at seven the next morning.

He almost expected her to stay to argue about the earliness of the hour of departure, but to his relief, she curtsied and left.

Yvonne lay awake for a long time, listening to the tremendous noise and bustle in the inn.

Doors kept opening and shutting and bells ringing. Voices cried to the waiter from every corner, while he cried back, "Coming!" while going on to serve someone else. Everybody was in a hurry, preparing for embarkation on one of the packets or just arriving, and impatient to be on the homeward road. Every now and then a carriage would rattle up to the door at a tremendous speed, making the whole inn shake. The man who cleaned the boots was running in one direction, and the barber with his powder bag in the other, while the din of porters and sailors taking in luggage or taking it out rose up from the hall. A horn blew, announcing the arrival of the post, and then, later, another blast, signaling its departure.

"This is better than I thought," mused Yvonne, lying in bed with her hands clasped behind her head. A picture of the viscount's face rose before her eyes.

"*Much* better!"

Chapter Two

Yvonne had breakfasted and dressed and was waiting outside the inn by seven in the morning. She had a pleasurable feeling of anticipation. In front of her lay a drive through the English countryside with the viscount at her side.

To her fury, the footman who had met her at the customs house the day before appeared to say that his lordship had gone ahead in a post chaise to prepare for her ladyship's arrival.

The fact was that the viscount had decided he could not bear Yvonne's pert and upsetting company on the road home. By the time she arrived, Miss Cottingham would be there and he would not have to trouble very much about Yvonne again.

Yvonne felt the snub keenly and retaliated by insisting Gustave travel inside the carriage with her.

The disapproving footman shut the carriage door on the pair of them, listening with even more disapproval to the stream of voluble French coming from inside.

At last Yvonne finished complaining to Gustave about the viscount's ungentlemanly treatment and settled back to enjoy the journey. Unlike Portuguese coaches, this one was not closed in by curtains but had glass on either side, which afforded a good view of the countryside.

Although it was late April, there was only a faint tinge of green on the trees. Everything had a cold and coarse appearance, and the hedge plants looked mean and insignificant — nettles, thistles, and thorns — to eyes accustomed to the aloe, acanthus, arbitus, and vine. Dreary stretches lay on either side, and black clouds with trailing fingers of rain moved across the sullen scene.

It was very cold. Yvonne's spirits took a plunge.

Gustave appeared sunk in gloom.

"What is to become of me, milady?" he asked at last. "That *serviteur* said there was no place in milord's household for me."

"Your place is as my servant," snapped Yvonne. "Do not be stupid, Gustave. If they do not let you stay, then I shall run off with you and we shall live as the gypsies."

Gustave shivered and cracked his bony knuckles. "I would not make a good gypsy, milady. I am old and used to sleeping in a house."

"Well, do not trouble yourself. You stay with me."

Yvonne gradually dropped off to sleep, lulled

by the rocking of the carriage and the monotony of the landscape.

Gustave finally awoke her. "I think," he said in tones of deepest foreboding, "that we are nearly at our destination."

Yvonne looked out of the window. "Oh, dear," she said.

Yellow, hideous, and sinister, Trewent Castle loomed up on the edge of the cliffs, overlooking the sea. They drove through an archway cut into high walls topped with iron spikes.

Yvonne clutched Gustave. "He cannot live *here*," she gasped. "He is putting us in prison."

"Those are liveried servants moving about the grounds, not jailors," said Gustave.

The carriage came to a halt outside a massive iron-studded door.

The carriage steps were let down, and Yvonne alighted and gazed up in awe at the grim castle. There was not even any ivy on the walls to soften its uncompromising outline.

She could hear the pounding of the sea, and above her head a seagull let out a melancholy scream.

The footman rang the bell beside the door. It was a huge black iron bell on a rope. Yvonne put her hands over her ears to shut out its yammering, clanging sound.

The great double doors slowly opened, revealing a black hall like a cavern.

The elderly butler, Fairbairn, bowed before them. "My lord is in the library," he said.

Yvonne's spirits rose again. Soon she would be seated in front of a roaring fire, chatting with her handsome guardian.

The viscount was standing by one of the library windows, talking to a tall, elegant lady.

"Miss Cottingham," he said, "may I present your charge, Yvonne de la Falaise. Yvonne, Miss Cottingham. Make your curtsy."

Yvonne's lip curled in disdain. "If this Miss Cottingham is my governess, then *she* should curtsy to *me*. Furthermore, I prefer to be addressed by my title and treated with the courtesy due to my rank."

"While I am your guardian," said the viscount, "you will be treated exactly as I see fit. When, and if, we entertain company, your rank will be honored. Here you are Yvonne to Miss Cottingham and me."

Miss Cottingham came forward with a smile of welcome. "Since we are not to stand on ceremony," she said, "you may call me Patricia."

She held out her hand. Yvonne looked at it mulishly for a few seconds and then decided she was being churlish. "I am pleased to make your acquaintance, Patricia," she said demurely.

Tea was brought in and placed on a small table. Footmen carried chairs forward, and the viscount, the governess, and Yvonne arranged themselves about the tea tray. Most of the heat from an enormous fire in the huge hearth went straight up the chimney, leaving the room feeling cold and damp.

Miss Cottingham and the viscount talked about local people and local matters. It seemed, Yvonne reflected, that this Patricia had made it her business to find out much about the viscount's estates.

Still, she appeared a pleasant, friendly lady. Yvonne fought down a half-formed, half-understood wish that she might have the viscount all to herself and tried several times to join in the conversation. But they listened to her politely before returning eagerly to the subject they had been discussing before her interruption.

Yvonne grew more and more uneasy. Was this viscount married? He seemed to look with too much warmth and approval on this governess. She was only a servant, thought Yvonne huffily, as she helped herself to another cake and studied Patricia from under her lashes.

Patricia, it appeared, had arrived a bare half hour before Yvonne.

A housekeeper came in to say the ladies' rooms were ready. Patricia and Yvonne curtsied to the viscount and followed her out.

To Yvonne's amazement, Patricia's suite was on the same floor as her own and of the same size. Each had a bedroom, sitting room, and dressing room.

Patricia came to supervise the unpacking of Yvonne's many trunks. "Is his lordship married?" asked Yvonne.

"No, he is not," said Patricia. She turned to

the maid. "You must find another wardrobe for her ladyship's room. She has so many clothes."

"Are you married yourself?" asked Yvonne hopefully.

"No, I have never married. I could not act as your governess were I married."

"And how did you come by this post?"

"Lord Anselm put an advertisement in the local paper and I replied to it."

"Do you know why Lord Anselm comes to be my guardian?"

"Yes, he told me all about you before you arrived."

"His lordship seems to have formed a high opinion of you in a very short time. Did he tell you he was pleased to become my guardian?"

"He said he was legally entitled to refuse and might have considered doing so had he not found me to take care of you."

"No doubt you come with excellent references," said Yvonne in a thin little voice.

"Yes, I do have excellent references, but his lordship did not even trouble to read them," said Patricia with what Yvonne sharply and uncharitably thought was a trace of smugness.

Yvonne wanted to be alone. "See to your own unpacking, Patricia," she said. "I shall do very well now. Thank you," she added with an obvious effort.

Patricia left and Yvonne crossed to the window and looked out at the sea. The bedroom was very cold. Although it had obviously been painted very recently, there were already traces of damp up by the cornice.

"It is very damp," she said to one of the housemaids who was passing with her arms full of clothes.

"Yes, my lady," said the girl. "They say the sea comes right up in under the castle where the old dungeons used to be."

The housekeeper, Mrs. Pardoe, appeared in the doorway.

"Beg pardon, my lady, but his lordship would like to see you and Miss Cottingham in the library again."

"Thank you," said Yvonne, thinking quickly. "Do not trouble to inform Miss Cottingham. I shall tell her myself."

Delighted at the thought that she had engineered a way to see the viscount alone, Yvonne brushed her black curls and then ran lightly down the stairs to the library.

"Sit down, Yvonne," said the viscount. "We shall await Miss Cottingham."

"But in the meantime," said Yvonne, "you may as well tell me why you want to see me."

"It concerns your servant, Gustave."

"Gustave? Then it is *my* concern what becomes of him and mine alone. It has nothing to do with Miss Cottingham."

"I rely on her calm good sense," said the viscount repressively. "The problem is I have no need of an extra servant, and Gustave has not been trained in the ways of an English house-hold."

Now, the viscount had often been subjected to emotional blackmail, but never before had he faced such an expert as Yvonne.

She sank to her knees in front of him and clasped her hands. Her large eyes, lifted to his, swam with tears.

"Oh, my Gustave," she said in a choked voice. "So brave and so loyal, to be thrown out to fend for himself in a foreign land."

"Please rise," said the viscount, thoroughly alarmed. But Yvonne remained kneeling, a picture of wretched misery.

"There is much he could do. He could be my groom. I like riding."

The viscount's face cleared. "That would serve very well," he said. "Is he good with horses?"

"Oh, very good," lied Yvonne. She knew that Gustave was afraid of horses and could barely tell one end of the animal from the other.

Anselm leaned down and took her hands in a firm clasp and raised her to her feet. She staggered slightly and fell against his chest so that her black curls tickled his nose as he looked down at her. She raised glowing eyes to his face. "Thank you," she breathed. Then she stood on tiptoe and kissed him on the cheek.

"Your gratitude is excessive," said the viscount, backing away as if he had been stung.

The door opened and Patricia Cottingham walked in.

31

"Mrs. Pardoe, the housekeeper, informed me you wished to see me, my lord. She had already spoken to Yvonne, but Yvonne said she would inform me herself, and did not."

"La!" Yvonne laughed. "I forgot."

"Please leave us," said the viscount, and Yvonne looked hopefully at Patricia.

"No, I mean you, Yvonne. There is something I wish to say to Miss Cottingham."

Yvonne left but only went as far as the other side of the door, where she pressed her ear against the panels, not being weighed down by any stupid English inhibitions about not listening at doors to other people's conversation.

The panels of the door were very thick, and so Yvonne could only hear an indistinct murmur of voices. She stooped down and put her ear to the keyhole.

The voices were still too low. But perhaps they might soon speak louder.

"And as to the matter of my ward," the viscount was saying, "do you think you will be able to cope with her?"

"I do not like discussing your ward when she is listening at the door," said Patricia gently. "I did not hear her go upstairs."

"Surely not." The viscount strode to the door and jerked it open. Yvonne rose from her stooping position with a flaming face.

"I was tying the ribbons on my sandals," she gasped before flying up the stairs.

"Impossible child," said the viscount, shutting the door and turning once more to Patricia.

"She will soon become accustomed to our English ways," said Patricia placidly. "She must be overset with the excitement of the journey. It must also be a great strain for her to converse constantly in English. What was it you wished to discuss with me, my lord?"

"Simply the matter of what to do with Yvonne's French servant. But that has been settled."

Patricia nodded but did not say anything. Lord Anselm looked at her with approval. She never chattered on unnecessarily. Her fair hair was braided in a neat coronet on her head. Her dove-gray gown was simply cut but flattered the elegant lines of her body. She exuded an air of tranquillity and calm.

"As to arrangements for meals," said the viscount, "I have already endured one dinner in Yvonne's company and am reluctant to suffer another. I should like you both to take your meals in the little dining room. It is at the end of the corridor on the second floor, just along from your rooms. But provided I am not out and about on the estate, I should like you to meet me here at four o'clock each afternoon to give me your report."

"Certainly, my lord."

"As to Yvonne's education, she appears to think she knows everything. To keep her out of mischief, it might be as well to find something she does *not* know and occupy her mind with that."

"Yes, my lord."

"I think that is all, Miss Cottingham. You may go."

She dropped him a graceful curtsy and glided from the room.

Yvonne, dressed in her best silk gown, was furious when she learned she was to dine with her governess while the viscount dined apart. But she kept her temper. It was early days yet. She was determined the viscount should like and respect her, and taking her temper out on her governess was certainly not the way to achieve it.

After dinner, she said good night to Patricia, pleading exhaustion. But instead of going to bed, she put on a warm cloak and slipped downstairs.

She saw the butler, Fairbairn, crossing the hall and asked him where she might find Gustave.

"He has been given lodgings in the stables," said Fairbairn. "I shall send for him."

"No, I shall go myself."

Fairbairn looked at the great doors, which were already locked for the night. "I'll need to ask his lordship's permission to unlock the doors, my lady."

"No, do not do that," said Yvonne, turning away. "I can see Gustave in the morning."

Fairbairn bowed and left.

Yvonne stood in the shadowy hall, biting her lip. The viscount would simply forbid her to go out. But poor Gustave! Lodged in the stables. Sleeping on straw! There must be another way out of the castle. She found the back stairs, which led down to the kitchens, at the far corner of the hall. She followed the twisting stone staircase down and down.

She quietly pushed open the baize door to the kitchen. It was empty, and from a room beyond it came the sound of voices. The servants were obviously enjoying their own dinner in the servants' hall.

She slipped quietly across the kitchen and out a door on the other side and then through a chain of small rooms — butler's pantry, pantry, scullery — until she saw another door in front of her. She gently turned the key and let herself out into the night.

A great howling gale struck her, tearing at the skirts of her gown and tugging her hair free from its pins. She set out into the darkness, pausing every now and then to sniff the air for the smell of horses.

A hunter's moon sailed high above through the tearing clouds. The castle looked black and sinister and evil. The wind, shrieking through the battlements, sounded like the cries of condemned men.

She began to wish she had waited until morning.

Then she saw a dim figure over by some out-buildings and called out, "You, over there. Come here immediately."

The figure came closer, and by the fitful light of the moon, she saw he was wearing the Anselm outdoor livery.

"I am looking for my servant, Gustave," she said.

The man bowed. "Follow me, my lady."

Gratified that even the outdoor servants had heard of her and knew her title, Yvonne tripped after him. He led the way to the side of the castle, where the white disk of a stable clock shone in the moonlight.

Instead of going into the stables, he led the way to a staircase at the side. "It's up there, my lady," said the servant. "Second door. Would you like me to announce you?"

"No, thank you. I can find the way myself."

She went up the staircase and found a narrow corridor at the top. She knocked at the second door, and Gustave opened it.

"Come in, my lady," he said, standing aside.

Yvonne walked in and looked about her curiously.

It was a small, cozy room lit by an oil lamp. There was a narrow bed covered with a patchwork quilt, a small fireplace, a table, and two chairs. There were chintz curtains at the window and even a blue hooked rug on the floor.

"This is very fine, Gustave," said Yvonne. "When I heard you had been sent to the stables, I was afraid you were lying in straw."

"It *is* very good," said Gustave. "I am to be your personal groom. You will not tell them I detest the horses?"

"No. Gustave, of course not. Are the other servants kind to you?"

"They do not like foreigners; that is plain. But I think they have been ordered to look after me. I have been supplied with tobacco, beer, and coals for the fire."

"He is very kind, this guardian of mine," said Yvonne, sitting at the table.

"Yes, milady."

"Just the kind of man Papa would have wished me to marry."

"Just so, milady. I have very few words of English, but I understand more than I can speak. One of the old grooms was in the wars and speaks a little of our language, so I put together that his lordship is not married because he once had many lady relatives in his charge.

"He says he detests the women, all of them. He has not smiled once" — Gustave looked at her slyly — "before the arrival of this governess."

A shadow crossed Yvonne's face. "Ah, the so excellent Miss Cottingham. So sensible, so practical. But it is unthinkable that a lord should marry a servant."

"This governess is not quite a servant. She has the distinction of being hired as your companion rather than as your governess, which elevates her in the eyes of the household. She has been talked about very much since her arrival today. The servants say it might not be a bad thing if his lordship married her."

Yvonne felt tired and depressed. "They talk a great deal of nonsense."

She stayed chatting to Gustave for some time, enjoying the freedom of being able to converse in her native tongue.

When she took her leave, the sky was cloudless and the moon was bright. She was able to find her way without difficulty.

Instead of going to the kitchen door, she went around the side of the castle and then out to the edge of the cliffs and looked down.

Far down below, the sea rose and fell, surging against the cliffs and dropping back. She leaned forward, thinking she saw the dark shape of a small boat very near the cliffs. If it was a boat, it would surely be sucked against the cliffs by the land swell.

"Yvonne!"

Startled, Yvonne nearly fell over. She whipped about and clutched at a sleeve.

"What are you doing out here?" demanded Patricia Cottingham.

"What are *you* doing out here?" countered Yvonne crossly.

"I came looking for you. Let us go in. You must never go so near the edge of the cliffs again. It is most dangerous."

"I think there is a boat right down there," said Yvonne, turning back to the sea. "They will surely be dashed against the cliffs."

"Nonsense," said Patricia sharply. "If you do not return with me *this minute,* I shall be forced to tell Lord Anselm of your escapade, and then your freedom will be much curtailed. Besides, there is no boat there."

"How do you know? You have not even looked."

"I do not need to look. I know this coast. No boat would come so close to the cliffs."

"Then I am going to show you," said Yvonne, giving her an impatient little push. "Look! There!"

Yvonne blinked. The sea rose and fell, silver and empty under the moon.

"You see," said Patricia calmly, "you have been imagining things. Do you come with me now, or do I have to call Lord Anselm?"

"Oh, very well," said Yvonne, beginning to walk back toward the castle. "But there *was* a boat. I *saw* it."

Chapter Three

The next month turned out to be the weariest and most boring time Yvonne had ever endured.

The viscount owned property in the north and had left four days after her arrival at Trewent Castle with only a curt good-bye.

The weather was miserable. The sea pounded on the rocks, and great buffets of wind hurtled hail against the leaded windows of the castle.

Yvonne, left in the company of Patricia Cottingham, tried to make the best of things. She dimly suspected her companion's education was sadly deficient, but then it was very hard to find out what Patricia did know or did not know.

Patricia questioned Yvonne closely as to *her* education and then suggested she study science. Yvonne, intrigued at being allowed to study a subject normally considered a masculine preserve, readily agreed. Patricia ordered books from Truro and then seemed content to sit and sew while Yvonne studied them, occasionally remarking in her calm way, "Really! Yes, it is fascinating, is it not?" when Yvonne read something out to her.

Gustave bravely faced the weather and his fear of horses to accompany Yvonne riding. Yvonne had chosen a mount for him, to the amusement of the stable staff — an old and placid mare. Gustave was delighted. He said it was just like riding an animated sofa.

Patricia said she disliked riding and did not accompany them. She tried, however, to get Yvonne to wear a mask, saying her skin would become sadly weatherbeaten. Yvonne refused. Patricia remarked casually that a man as fair as Lord Anselm would surely not admire a lady with a tanned and leathery skin, and so Yvonne compromised by wearing a veil.

And then when the horrible month of May was over, when everyone had quite decided there would be no spring at all, the weather changed abruptly. The skies cleared and the sun shone down. Flowers and green leaves appeared all over the place as if by magic. The castle windows were opened to let in the sunny, fresh air.

A letter arrived from Lord Anselm. He was near the end of his journey, he said, and would be with them soon.

Yvonne tore gown after gown out of her closets, trying on first one and then another. Her hair had grown very long. Would he like it shorter? Would he even notice her? Would he see her at all, or would he send for Patricia and leave her alone in her rooms?

She heard the sounds of his arrival two days later and waited impatiently for his summons.

She heard a servant mounting the stairs, but he scratched at Patricia's sitting room door and not at Yvonne's.

Yvonne heard Patricia descending the stairs, and then there was silence.

Her eyes filled with tears. Was she so very repulsive that he did not even want to see her?

Tired of sitting in her room, she walked down the stairs and looked longingly at the library door. Then she walked out of the castle and went around to the front.

There was a very small stretch of grass between the castle and the cliff's edge. Under the library windows ran a terrace.

After some hesitation, Yvonne quietly mounted the steps to the terrace and edged her way along to the nearest library window.

It was open and she could hear their voices clearly. Lord Anselm sounded very animated. He was describing his journey.

Yvonne leaned forward and peeped in.

Lord Anselm and Patricia were standing on either side of the fireplace. Patricia was wearing a gown Yvonne had not seen before. It was of pale blue silk. She stood with her eyes modestly lowered. Yvonne noticed the way the viscount's eyes lingered on her.

She felt a choking lump rise in her throat as she turned away.

She felt unloved and unwanted.

She went back up to her rooms and changed into her riding habit, and soon she was striding toward the stables, calling for Gustave.

She rode a great distance across the moors with Gustave on the old mare plodding behind her. At last, as the sun began to sink into the sea, Gustave called plaintively to say that he and his beast were exhausted.

Reluctantly, Yvonne wheeled her mount about and set out for the castle.

There were no instructions for her to see the viscount, only a placid dinner with Patricia as usual for company. Patricia did not remark on Yvonne's long absence but merely talked about the masons who had arrived that afternoon to set their ladders up outside the castle preparatory to repointing the brickwork.

"Lord Anselm tells me he plans to have the whole building redecorated," said Patricia. "He has been gracious enough to seek my advice as to colors and materials. He had our rooms painted before our arrival, but he is not satisfied with the result and wants them done again."

She turned her head to instruct a servant to take away their empty plates. Yvonne glared at her. She had learned from Gustave that afternoon that the servants, much as they approved of Patricia, had nonetheless been somewhat shocked that their master should immediately demand to see her and neglect his ward.

Yvonne began to wonder whether she really *liked* her guardian. He had snubbed her time after time, and he was beginning to shock his own servants by treating the governess like an equal.

Yvonne would have been even more wretched had she known her guardian was not deliberately snubbing her. Most of the time, he forgot about her very existence. Her only importance in his life at that moment was to supply him with an excuse to summon Miss Cottingham to interviews.

He was guiltily aware that in consulting the governess about the redecoration of his home, he was stepping out of line. But after years of giggling, dithering, shrieking females, it was wonderful to see Patricia's calm face and listen to her quiet, steady voice.

He finished an excellent dinner and, after going through the estate books, took himself off to bed, well content.

He would have been horrified and amazed could he have known that his little ward was lying facedown on her bed, crying her eyes out.

Yvonne became aware of someone in her bedroom. She struggled up against the pillows. The bed curtains were drawn back, and she saw Patricia standing there with a candle in one hand and a glass in the other.

"I heard you crying," said Patricia, "so I brought you some hot milk to help you sleep. What is the matter?"

"I hate this country," said Yvonne, scrubbing at her wet eyes with her fists. "I wish I were back in Portugal."

"The strangeness will soon wear off," said Patricia gently. "Drink your milk. It will soothe your poor nerves."

Yvonne drank the glass of milk and then said, "I am grateful to you for your sympathy, Patricia. I shall do very well now. Please leave me."

"Good night," said Patricia.

Yvonne stared miserably up at the bed canopy. Tomorrow she would do something, *anything,* to bring herself to her guardian's attention.

Abruptly, she fell into a deep sleep. In her dreams, she was once more in Lisbon, away from this cold, unfriendly England. The sun beat down on her head. She was warm. Beautifully warm. If she looked across, she could see the tall ships in the harbor and little fishing boats rocking at anchor. She found she could not see the Lisbon harbor clearly. She forced her eyes open, waking up as she did so. At first she thought her dream had changed for another one and that she was in the grip of a nightmare.

The wall of her room, over on the left-hand side, was a sheet of flame.

She leaped from her bed and fell on the floor. Her legs were strangely wobbly and would not seem to support her. She crawled to the door and pulled herself upright by hanging on to the handle. Then she turned the handle. The door would not open.

She screamed and battered at the door with her fists.

"Over here!" called a voice at the open window.

Eyes dilated with fear, Yvonne swung around. Patricia was at the open window, balancing precariously on the top rung of one of the stonemasons' ladders.

Yvonne tried to run to her, but once more her legs gave out. Patricia climbed through the window and, with surprising strength, hoisted Yvonne up and slung her over her shoulder. Then she made her way out of the window, and, crying to Yvonne to lie still, she began to edge her way down the ladder while the great fire bell of Trewent Castle beat on the still night air.

The viscount, roused from a deep sleep by the cries of his servants and the clamor of the bell, ran up the stairs toward the noise and shouting.

He, too, found it impossible to open Yvonne's door. "Try to break it down," he shouted to his servants. "The masons' ladders are outside. I shall try to reach her room from the outside."

And so it was that Lord Anselm reached the foot of the ladder just in time to witness Patricia's gallant rescue.

He was stunned with gratitude and admiration. How pale and brave Patricia looked when she set his ward on her feet. Yvonne promptly slumped on the ground and began to cry.

With infinite patience, Patricia soothed Yvonne and coaxed her into trying to take a few steps. Then with Patricia's strong arm about her waist, Yvonne was led around to the main door of the castle.

"Let me carry her," begged the viscount at one point, and shocked and groggy as she was, Yvonne gritted her teeth in fury as she heard Patricia's calm refusal.

She was led into a little-used morning room on the ground floor and laid on a sofa.

One of the servants came in to say that the door had not been locked after all but must have been jammed. They had heard someone call "Fire" from the other end of the corridor, and they had all run in that direction. When they had returned, having found no other fire, the door of Yvonne's room was lying open and they were able to extinguish the blaze. The fire had not spread to her ladyship's dressing room, so all of her clothes were safe. A writing desk, a commode, and a table had all been burned. An oil lamp had been found smashed on the floor. It must have been knocked over and started the fire.

"But I did not light the oil lamp," cried Yvonne, but Patricia said soothingly, "Shhh, my dear," and signaled to two stout house-maids to carry Yvonne upstairs again. A spare bedroom had been prepared for her, said Patricia, and she would be able to return to her own room in the morning after it had been cleaned and repaired.

To Yvonne, it was like being caught up in some weird dream. She could barely keep her eyes open.

As she was carried from the room, the last thing she saw was the glow of admiration in the viscount's eyes as he looked at Patricia.

Yvonne was kept in bed for the whole of the next day. She felt oddly weary and kept dropping off to sleep. By evening, after a light supper, she began to feel refreshed and settled back against the pillows to turn over the events of the fire in her mind. It had certainly been very brave of Patricia to rescue her. Who would have thought such a cool, elegant lady would have so much strength? Then there was the question of the oil lamp. It had definitely not been lit when she fell asleep. But was she sure? Yvonne remembered being wide awake one minute and plunged into sleep the next. Perhaps Patricia had put something in that glass of milk to make her sleep.

But the real source of Yvonne's worry was that she had shown herself to the viscount to be little more than a careless girl who might have burned his house down about his ears. In comparison, Patricia must seem like a paragon of all the virtues.

Yvonne began to resent Patricia, although chiding herself all the while for her uncharitable thoughts. Patricia had saved her life.

Before she fell asleep again, Yvonne decided to put her silly feelings about the governess away and concentrate on some way of seeing her guardian alone.

Next day, after haunting the hall between study periods — for self-education could hardly be called lessons — Yvonne decided to hide in the library behind a Chinese lacquered screen that stood in one corner.

The library was the viscount's favorite room. Yvonne planned to stay in hiding until she heard him come in. She would pretend to have fallen asleep. That way she would be able to see him alone.

But Yvonne had forgotten about the viscount's regular four o'clock meeting with Patricia. She had been hiding behind the screen when she heard him come in. She was about to yawn loudly and affect to have just woken up when she heard Patricia's voice and the swish of her long skirts over the floor.

"Good afternoon, Miss Cottingham," Yvonne heard the viscount say. "How is that wretched child?"

"She has made a good recovery," replied Patricia. "We have been studying more science today."

"Excellent. Yvonne is fortunate in having so highly educated a governess to teach her. Miss

Cottingham, I cannot begin to express my gratitude for your bravery — for having saved Yvonne's life."

"I was only glad to be of assistance, my lord."

"But what courage! What resourcefulness! *You* put your own life at risk. Let us hope there will be no more frights and alarms caused by that headstrong little girl. I shall be very glad when she finally marries."

"Then what will become of me, my lord?" Patricia's clear voice held a note of teasing, of flirtation.

"You have a home here for as long as you want," said the viscount.

"I cannot possibly stay here alone with you," said Patricia. "It would occasion much gossip."

Yvonne pressed one eye to the hinge of the screen.

Patricia was standing with her hands clasped, her head turned slightly away from the viscount. He was studying her averted face.

He took one step toward her. "You could stay as . . ."

But the rest of his words were lost in one almighty crash as Yvonne toppled the screen over.

Yvonne did not like the expression in her guardian's eyes. Never before had any man looked at her with such dislike.

"Enough," snapped the viscount. "Leave us."

But Yvonne was not going to leave him alone with Patricia. She was not going to allow him to finish the sentence he had started. As far as

Yvonne was concerned, there could only be one ending to that sentence, and it went, "as my wife."

She put her hand to her forehead and swayed toward Patricia. "I feel faint," whispered Yvonne. "I fear I am not yet fully recovered."

"Oh, take her away, for goodness' sake." The viscount sighed. "We will speak further, Miss Cottingham."

Yvonne felt the arm Patricia put about her to assist her from the room was unnecessarily tight.

Once in her own sitting room, Yvonne pretended to make a quick recovery.

"May I leave you?" asked Patricia. "I have things to do."

Yvonne bit her lip. She felt sure one of the things Patricia meant to do was to return to the library and get the viscount to finish that sentence.

But she could not think of anything to say to detain her. Patricia went along to her own sitting room, but Yvonne was sure the governess was only going to stay long enough to arrange her hair before going down to the library.

Panic seized Yvonne. She did not want her guardian to marry Patricia. She did not know why. All she knew at that moment was that the whole idea was abhorrent to her.

A diversion! She must create a diversion. The fire bell. Where was it? She remembered one of the maids saying it was in the cellars.

She slipped along the corridor. Patricia was

singing as she moved about her sitting room.

Yvonne darted down the main staircase and then down the back stairs. There were noises coming from the kitchen, the clatter of dishes and the sizzling of roast meat. If only these stairs went on down to the cellars. There was no way she could possibly get through the kitchen unobserved.

The stairs went on, down and down, until she found herself confronted by a stout oaken door. To her relief, she saw a key in it and turned it. The hinges of the door were well oiled, and it opened without a sound. A candle and a tin-derbox stood on a barrel just inside the door.

Tinderboxes usually seemed possessed of the devil and sometimes would take as much as twenty minutes to supply a light, but this one worked almost immediately. Holding the candle in its flat stick, Yvonne flitted quickly through serried rows of barrels and wine bottles. Where on earth was the fire bell? She was about to give up when she saw a long rope dangling in a far corner. Of course! The bell itself would not be in the cellars but somewhere up on the roof. She ran to the rope and looked up. Far, far above her head was the black mouth of the fire bell surrounded by a small square of blue sky — too far away to affect the temperature of the cellar below.

She put down the candle, seized the rope, and gave an almighty pull.

Upstairs, Patricia paused with her hand on

the handle of the library door as the fire bell began to sound. The door swung open and the viscount almost collided with her.

"Outside!" he commanded. "Make sure everyone is outside."

Downstairs in the cellars, Yvonne gave the rope a final pull and then made her way toward where she remembered the door to be. And then she heard footsteps coming down the cellar stairs.

She blew out the candle and crouched down behind a barrel against the far wall.

The voice of Fairbairn, the butler, reached her ears. "I know there's no fire," he was muttering. "We was all in the kitchens, so who's been ringing that bell?"

The butler was carrying a branch of candles. "Whoever you are," called Fairbairn, "I'll find you. I'm locking us both in." Yvonne heard a click as he locked the cellar door. "I know every inch of these cellars, so you shan't escape me."

Yvonne felt her mouth grow dry with fear. If Fairbairn found her, then she would be dragged before the viscount. He might be so angry, he would send her away.

The glow from the branch of candles held by the butler grew brighter and brighter.

Yvonne pressed back against the wall. It seemed to give a little. She pressed harder. What she was pressing against appeared to be not the wall but a piece of wood or a small door. She twisted about and pushed with all her might. She could not see, but she felt what must be a small door swing open, and she crept through on her hands and knees, feeling her way in the blackness with the tips of her fingers. It was as well she did not straighten up, for all at once her groping hands encountered nothing. She felt lower and found she was at the head of a flight of stone stairs.

Not wanting to venture farther in the blackness, she stayed where she was, hoping Fairbairn did not know of this strange exit.

After waiting a long time, she cautiously made her way back, feeling on the cellar floor for the candle and tinderbox. She waited again, listening, wondering if Fairbairn was lying low, trying to trick her by keeping quiet.

But the oppressive blackness of the place pressed on her nerves. She decided to light the candle.

This time the tinderbox took its time in producing a flame. By the time the candle was lit, Yvonne was frightened and thoroughly ashamed of herself. She turned to check the door through which she had groped her way. It was not really a door but a piece of wood covered with sacking placed over a small hole. She held the candle higher and found the sacking had been daubed with gray paint to make it blend in with the stone of the walls and pasted onto the wood.

Perhaps the prisoners had used this way as an escape in the old days, thought Yvonne with a shiver. She hoped Fairbairn had not locked the cellar door. She dreaded having to explore the blackness of the secret way.

To her immeasurable relief, the cellar door had not been locked. When she reached the kitchen level, she listened hard but could not hear a sound.

She poked her head around the kitchen door. No one. She made her way out of the castle by the same route she had taken when she had first gone to look for Gustave.

By the noise coming from outside, she gathered that everyone was still assembled on the lawn in front of the castle.

She crept around a corner of the building. Everyone was listening to Fairbairn, who was telling them the bell must have been rung by the ghost of Black Jack, the pirate, who was said to haunt the old dungeons that were half covered by the sea under the castle.

Yvonne strolled over and stood at the back of the crowd. No one noticed her.

"Tish, man," came the viscount's voice. "I do not believe in ghosts or phantoms or rubbish like that. Where is my ward?"

"Here, my lord," called Yvonne sweetly. The crowd parted to let her through.

The viscount looked relieved. Beside him stood Patricia Cottingham. For one brief moment before she lowered her eyes, Patricia looked at Yvonne.

And Yvonne saw suspicion in those eyes, suspicion and the beginnings of dislike.

Chapter Four

The next day dawned sunny and warm. The sea stretched out below the castle like watered silk.

"I wish you liked riding," said Yvonne with a sigh, pushing away her books. "All you ever seem to do, Patricia, is go out for walks in the middle of the night."

"What do you mean?" The needle that Patricia held in one well-shaped hand stopped flashing neatly through the tambour frame.

"I awoke in the middle of the night and went to your room," said Yvonne. "Your bed had not even been slept in."

"What did you want?"

Yvonne hesitated. What she had really wanted had been to find out whether Patricia had received a proposal of marriage from the viscount, something that now, in the clear light of day, she felt she could not ask her.

"I could not sleep," she said. "I awoke at two in the morning and could not get back to sleep. I thought that perhaps you could give me some laudanum or whatever it was you put in my milk on the night of the fire."

"I put nothing in your milk." The needle began to flash again as Patricia embroidered a Jacobean design of curved leaves and fruit. "I went down to the kitchens during the night to make myself some tea. I could not sleep either."

"Have you always disliked riding?" asked Yvonne.

"It is not that I particularly dislike it," said Patricia. "I do not ride well, and I do not show to advantage in the saddle."

Yvonne shifted restlessly. Now that the weather had turned fine, she could not bear to waste the whole day indoors with her books. "We could go for a walk," she suggested without much enthusiasm.

Patricia stabbed her needle into the tambour frame and walked to the window of Yvonne's sitting room. "I can row," she said over her shoulder.

"Do let us go down to the village, Patricia," begged Yvonne. "I am sure we could hire a boat."

"There is no need to do that." Patricia smiled. "There is a little rowing boat belonging to the castle. About half a mile along the cliffs from the main door, there is a winding path that descends the cliffs. The boat is tied to a jetty at the foot of the path. I shall take you there if you would like."

"I should like it above all things." Yvonne

laughed. "What shall we wear?"

"Something old and serviceable. We do not want our good gowns to become stained with saltwater."

Yvonne was delighted at the prospect of the outing.

As she set out along the cliffs with Patricia, she felt a rush of affection for the older woman.

She had misread that look in Patricia's eyes the day before. I have become jealous, thought Yvonne ruefully, and all because of a pompous guardian who does not even like me.

As the castle fell behind them, Yvonne felt the image of the viscount that she always seemed to carry in her head dwindle away to nothing. It was not that she was even in love with him, she told herself. It was more as if she had become obsessed with gaining his approval.

The path down to the jetty was steep with a few rough steps hacked out of chunks of rock to make the descent easier.

Sea pinks blew in the wind from tussocks of rough grass, and seagulls sailed overhead, hardly moving their wings.

There was the boat, just as Patricia had promised, with Trewent Castle painted in scarlet letters on its side.

"How did you discover it?" cried Yvonne.

"Walking," said Patricia with a laugh. "It is one of the advantages of not riding. One finds so many interesting places and things."

Again, Yvonne was impressed by Patricia's

strength as the governess took the oars and began to row with steady strokes away from the shore.

Patricia then let Yvonne take the oars, and both ladies fell about laughing as Yvonne kept sending the boat around in circles.

Yvonne was so absorbed in trying to learn to row properly and Patricia was so intent in watching that she did not drop one of the oars over the side that they did not see or hear the approach of the other boat until it was almost upon them.

Yvonne let out a sudden scream of terror, and Patricia twisted about to see what had alarmed her.

A larger rowing boat than theirs was coming alongside. In it were six men brandishing wicked-looking knives. They wore masks that appeared to have been made out of old bits of material. The leader had a long black beard.

"Get in our boat," growled the leader, "or we'll slit your throats."

"Don't kill us," pleaded Yvonne. "*Dieu!* We are but two defenseless women."

"Do as they say," said Patricia, her voice as calm and steady as ever.

Yvonne was hauled roughly into the other boat. She barked her shins on the gunwale and let out a whimper of pain.

"Stow it," said one of the men roughly, "or we'll throw you o'er the side."

And then there was a cry from the men as

Patricia suddenly dived neatly and swiftly over the side. Yvonne, despite her terror, watched in admiration as Patricia struck out strongly for the shore.

"Get help!" screamed Yvonne.

The men began to mutter to one another in a tongue Yvonne did not understand. They seemed to be debating what to do next. Yvonne strained her eyes, watching Patricia's head as the governess swam farther and farther away. "Please let her make it," prayed Yvonne.

The black-bearded leader said something and pointed along the coast and his men picked up the oars.

"What are you going to do with me?" pleaded Yvonne, but they rowed steadily, towing the Trewent Castle boat behind, and did not reply.

Soon they began to approach the shore about two miles south of the castle. Yvonne could see several caves, black holes in the white chalk of the cliffs.

"I have no money," said Yvonne, trying again. "It is of no use holding me for ransom."

Silence.

"Will no one speak to me?" demanded Yvonne, anger beginning to chase out fear.

In her mounting fury, she struck out at the oarsman nearest her. The leader said something. The crew shipped the oars. Yvonne's hands were tied behind her back, and then they started to row again.

Yvonne wished she could swim. But even had she been able to and even had she tried to escape before her hands were tied, it would have proved almost impossible, since she was wedged between two of the oarsmen in the middle of the boat.

Nearer the shore they drew, until the tall shadow of the looming cliffs blotted out the sun. The men rowed swiftly, straight into the mouth of a large cave. The tide was low, and the boat grated onto a beach of shingle.

Yvonne was ordered out. Then hands seized her, and she was dragged to an old wooden post that had obviously been used for tying up boats.

She was tied to the post, and then, without a word, the men got back into their boat and began to row quickly away.

Yvonne screamed for help until she was hoarse. And then she noticed the grave peril in which she stood.

The tide had turned, and greedy little waves were beginning to lap at her feet.

She twisted around and tried to see if the post would be covered at high tide, but her arms were too tightly bound behind her to allow her to turn very much.

She tried to cry for help again, but her voice was reduced to a broken whisper with all her shouting.

And then she heard her name called in a high, clear voice.

Summoning up the last of her energies, Yvonne threw back her head and screamed.

With a surge of hope she heard an answering call and then the steady sound of oars.

Tears of relief poured down Yvonne's face as a boat hove into view.

In it were Patricia, the viscount, four servants from the castle, and her own servant, Gustave.

The viscount was rowing and had taken off his coat. In his frilled cambric shirt and knee breeches, with his golden hair ruffled by the wind, he looked a romantic figure. But for once, Yvonne's only thoughts were of gratitude.

He was the first to leap from the boat. As he untied her, Yvonne fell sobbing into his arms. He cradled her against his chest, murmuring to her that she was safe, and, feeling the warmth and strength of his body, Yvonne indeed felt safe and loved.

All too quickly, she was surrendered to Patricia's care. And although Yvonne clung to Patricia, gasping broken thanks, she felt young and frightened and wished the viscount would put his arms around her again.

Then Yvonne discovered that Patricia's gown was still wet. "Yes," said the viscount, hearing her exclamation of distress. "Miss Cottingham refused to stay behind and change. She is the bravest and most courageous lady I have ever met."

And, oh, how tenderly those beautiful blue eyes of his smiled on Patricia, and, oh, how low and mean Yvonne felt as a great surge of jealousy washed over her.

She sat beside Gustave in the boat and answered his rapid questions, feeling it almost odd to speak in her native tongue. For Yvonne had even begun to think in English.

Once back at the castle, the worthies of Trewent village, along with the captain of the local militia, were waiting to question both Yvonne and Patricia. Patricia flashed Yvonne a look of concern and said that she herself would answer all questions. It was imperative Lady de la Falaise be put to bed.

Yvonne smiled weakly. She was shivering with shock and reaction.

"I shall carry her up," said the viscount. "No, I do not need any help. She is little more than a child."

Patricia would have followed them, but the viscount said, "Answer the questions these gentlemen put to you, Miss Cottingham, as quickly as possible. I am concerned for your health. You must change out of your wet clothes."

Then he picked Yvonne up in his arms. She gave a little sigh and leaned her head against his chest. He looked down at her flushed face and at those ridiculously long eyelashes fanned out over her cheeks. "Yvonne of the cliffs — that is what your name means."

"I know," said Yvonne, wishing he would go on carrying her forever. "How did you find me?"

"The redoubtable Miss Cottingham. She seems to have amassed a surprising knowledge of the coast in a very quick time. She had also watched where the men were taking you from the top of the cliffs. Once more, you owe her your life."

"Yes," agreed Yvonne, feeling very sinful and wicked because she could not manage to feel more grateful. "Do you have many brigands along this coast?"

"I believe a certain amount of smuggling goes on, but I have never heard of such a thing before. Why should a party of armed brigands attack two defenseless females? Did they say anything that might help us find out who they were?"

"No," said Yvonne. "They were speaking in some language I could not understand."

"Possibly Cornish. It is something like Breton."

"It was very frightening. But now that I think about it, it was all like a bad play. Do you think some of the locals might have dressed up like brigands to give us a fright?"

"Not when their capture means hanging," said the viscount grimly. "Everyone knows everyone else around here. My servants cannot think who they might be."

He carried her into her sitting room and placed her gently on a chair. "Is your bedroom repaired?" he said.

"Yes," said Yvonne. "You know, I cannot

think how that fire started. I did not have the oil lamp lit at all."

"You must go to sleep," he said, smoothing her ruffled hair with a gentle hand. He rang the bell for the housekeeper. "Mrs. Pardoe and her maids will put you to bed," he said. "Sleep well, infant."

"I am *not* an infant. I am a woman."

"Of course you are." The viscount laughed and deposited a careless kiss on the tip of her nose.

Mrs. Pardoe arrived just as he was leaving. She summoned two maids, and together they undressed Yvonne and bathed her and put her to bed.

After they had left, Yvonne fell asleep, but only for half an hour. She awoke and sat up.

Now Patricia would marry Lord Anselm. That was the first awful thought that flooded into Yvonne's brain.

He would admire her the more after this last adventure. How could *any* woman be so brave? She had leaped from that boat without a backward glance. One of the men could easily have swum after her and knifed her.

Why hadn't they?

Yvonne shook her head as if to clear it. All at once she felt she must talk to Gustave.

She dressed quickly and made her way out of the castle through the kitchen, explaining to the startled staff that she had lost her way.

Yvonne felt sure that had she gone out

through the main door, the viscount or Patricia would have seen her and called her back.

She ran lightly in the direction of the stables.

Gustave was not in his room. Yvonne saw a stable boy crossing the yard and called to him.

The boy came up to her, grinning awkwardly and wiping his hands on a sackcloth apron. "Where is my servant, Gustave?" demanded Yvonne.

"Over there, my lady," said the stable boy. He raised his arm and pointed in the direction of the tack room.

But Yvonne did not look in the direction of his pointing finger. She was staring at his arm. The boy was bare-armed, his shirtsleeves rolled back. The late sun shone on that youthful, tanned arm — a *boy's* arm.

The bearded "captain" of the brigands had had just such a youthful-looking arm . . . too youthful an arm to go with that enormous black beard. Yvonne frowned.

"How old are you?" she asked.

The boy blushed and tugged his forelock. "Sixteen, my lady."

"Sixteen! You are very young," said Yvonne from the lofty height of nearly eighteen years of age.

She hurried off in the direction of the tack room, leaving the stable boy staring after her.

Gustave was polishing horse brasses. He rose to his feet as Yvonne entered.

"Walk with me a little, Gustave," said

66

Yvonne. "I need to talk."

With his usual slow and deliberate movements, Gustave carefully put the cleaning materials away while Yvonne waited impatiently. Then mistress and servant began to walk toward the gate in the castle walls. Soon they were out on the moors.

The sun was setting over the sea. A light breeze tugged at the muslin skirts of Yvonne's gown and blew tendrils of black hair across her face.

"Now, Gustave," she said, "there are many things troubling me. The leader of the brigands had a long, black, dusty beard, but he had arms like a young man or boy, smooth and tanned. The next thing is this. When Patricia so bravely leaped overboard to swim for help, not one of them really tried to stop her. They could have jumped after her or rowed after her and caught her by her gown with the boat hook. And how did she know where to find me? Did you search all the caves?"

"No," said Gustave slowly. "But miss said she had been watching from the top of the cliffs and pretty much knew where they had taken you."

"That is what Lord Anselm said. But do you not think that I did not constantly scan the cliffs looking for help? I did, and I saw no one."

"What you are trying to say is that this governess deliberately arranged the whole thing," said Gustave patiently. "But why?"

"So that Lord Anselm will fall in love with her. He is already much admiring of her because of her bravery at the fire. Ah, the fire! I tell you, Gustave, that fire was most odd. It could not have been burning very long and yet Patricia managed to get out of the castle and up that ladder. And my door *was* locked. And another thing. I swear she drugged me first."

"But I have seen this lady, you forget!" exclaimed Gustave. "She is very English, prim and proper. Perhaps it is merely the strangeness of this foreign land playing tricks on your nerves, milady."

"If only I could be sure . . ." Yvonne stopped walking. "I could find out where Lord Anselm has put her references. Then I could travel to see her previous employers. If I can find her out in just one lie, surely the rest follows."

"Where will you find the money to travel anywhere?" asked Gustave.

"I have the last of the money left from the sale of the furniture. I already tried to give you some, but you refused."

"I no longer have need of money," said Gustave. "I am well paid here."

"That is another thing," said Yvonne. "If I go to find out about Patricia, you must remain here. No! *I* may only receive a stern reprimand, but it is more than likely that *you* would lose your job."

"I think you are mistaken about this governess," said Gustave. "Perhaps milady is a little jealous, *hein?* Do not do this. Think! Who suggested you should go rowing?"

Yvonne frowned. "Well, Patricia said she could row, and I asked her. . . ." Her voice trailed away.

"You see," said Gustave with satisfaction. "She could not have arranged the whole thing."

"But perhaps she is very clever," said Yvonne stubbornly. "I always get restless just about that time of day. I always want to go out. Usually Patricia prefers to stay and sew, so I go riding with you. She must have known I would jump at the chance of going out in a boat."

"Ladies do not usually show a marked enthusiasm for going out in boats," Gustave pointed out.

"Ah, not in Lisbon. But these Englishwomen are like Amazons."

"But *you* are not English. She could not know you would want to learn to row."

"But she could have allowed for that," cried Yvonne. "Suppose we had merely gone for a walk. Patricia could have led us down to the beach. These men could have been told to watch for us. They could just as easily have attacked us on the shore."

Gustave looked at his mistress gravely. "His lordship is too old for you," he said.

Yvonne flushed to the roots of her hair. "I am discussing my supposed capture. What do you mean?"

"You force me to point out, milady, that you

wish his lordship for yourself, which is why you want to find the governess at fault. You told me yourself he was just the sort of man your father would have wished you to marry."

"I am surprised at you, Gustave," snapped Yvonne. "I was merely funning when I said that. My guardian has been most kind to us *both*. If Patricia is innocent, then she has nothing to fear from me."

She turned and ran away, back to the castle.

Gustave watched her sadly until her slight figure was swallowed up in the black shadow of the castle walls.

Lord Anselm found sleep did not come easily that night. The events of the day had upset him. Yvonne would have been surprised to learn that Patricia's apparent heroics had not sparked tender feelings in the viscount's bosom. He was beginning to find such resourcefulness and bravery in a woman somewhat intimidating. The Patricia on the night of the fire had managed to appear calm and womanly throughout. The Patricia who had appeared dripping seawater in the hall of the castle and rapping out orders had been someone to admire — but not cherish. She had delivered her orders like a man — yes, as a man used to command! Did he really want to marry a lady simply because she was brave? The viscount was at that dangerous stage of life when men suddenly make up their minds to marry and usually settle for the nearest and most available female, since the motive is not love but a desire for sons. He was glad now that Yvonne had interrupted his proposal. He would wait and see.

He punched his pillow and tried to compose himself for sleep. Then he heard a light footfall on the stairs. He got out of bed, went to the door of his room, and gently opened it.

A bobbing circle of candlelight was descending the stairs. He could not make out who was holding the candle.

He picked up a silk dressing gown and wrapped it around his naked body. Then he went down the stairs, stopping every now and then to listen. He heard a creak as a door was opened. He knew that particular creak. The hinges of the library door needed oiling.

He walked across the hall. The library door had been left ajar, and there was the soft glow of candlelight streaming out into the hall.

He crept to the door of the library and looked in.

Yvonne de la Falaise was sitting at his desk, reading something. He strode quickly into the room and snatched the papers out of her hand.

"How dare you read my correspondence!" he said in an angry whisper.

Yvonne sat stricken.

The viscount lit an oil lamp and then studied the papers she had been reading. They were Patricia's references.

"What on earth were you doing with these?" he demanded.

"I was disturbed because I find Patricia's educational qualifications are not as high as she would have us believe."

"She is teaching you *science,* a subject of which most women are entirely ignorant."

"I am teaching *myself* science," said Yvonne hotly. "Patricia merely bought me the books and sits and sews while I study."

"You are a jealous little cat," said the viscount roundly. "Oh, never fear, I know you are not jealous because you entertain any tender feelings toward me. You are simply a spoiled child who wants all the attention. How can you? Miss Cottingham has already saved your life on two occasions. Is this how you thank her?"

Yvonne bit her lip. To say that she had come to doubt both happenings — the fire and the capture — would make her sound even worse. She remained silent.

"Go to bed," snapped the viscount. "We shall not distress poor Miss Cottingham by telling her of your disgraceful disloyalty and ingratitude."

Yvonne trailed miserably to the door. The viscount eyed her with disfavor. She was wearing quite the most frivolous nightgown he had ever seen.

"And if you must wander about the castle at night," he called after her, "for goodness' sake, put some clothes on!"

The only answer was the slamming of the library door.

Perhaps he would take her to London the following year, thought the viscount. Many men would wish to marry her. Those huge eyes and midnight-black hair would seduce any man not as hardened to the female sex as he was himself.

Chapter Five

A disgraceful old carriage swayed and rumbled over the stony country roads, driven by a coachman who looked as ancient and battered as his vehicle.

But Yvonne was content. She had made her escape from the castle by riding off before dawn. At the nearest town, Penryn, she had stabled her horse and hired the only carriage available, which belonged to the driver, Mr. Tom Bodkin. There was a prizefight in the neighborhood, and all of the best carriages and gigs had been rented.

Yvonne had not been able to memorize the address of Mrs. Benham in Exeter, but she had been able to memorize the name and address on Patricia's other reference — Mrs. Paxton, Corby Hall, Truro.

She hoped to reach Truro before midday. The old horse pulled the old carriage so slowly that at times Yvonne thought she would be better to get down and walk.

The day was too bright. A yellow glaring light flooded the moors.

At times Yvonne thought uneasily of the con-
sternation her disappearance might cause if she
stayed away too long. Yvonne promised the
gods that if Patricia's reference should prove
valid, then she would bow to the inevitable and
let Patricia have the viscount.

By the time they reached Truro, it was two in
the afternoon.

"Where do you want to be set down, miss?"
called the coachman.

Yvonne lowered the glass and stuck her head
out. Truro looked a pleasant, prosperous town.
The overhanging buildings shut out the omi-
nous darkening of the sky to the west.

"I think I shall walk," said Yvonne, impatient
to get out of the smelly old carriage.

She climbed down from the carriage, and the
coachman heaved his great bulk down from the
box.

"I shall meet you at that inn over there," said
Yvonne, pointing to a hostelry called the Three
Feathers.

"I think miss ought to be a-paying me half
the fare," said the coachman.

"Oh, very well," said Yvonne crossly. She
paid the driver and then set out along the main
street of Truro. The shops were very fine, and
she was so engrossed in examining all the wares
displayed in their windows that it was some
time before she realized her appearance was oc-
casioning comment.

The people of Truro had never before seen

such a beautiful and fashionably dressed young lady alone and on foot. Yvonne was wearing a dashing riding dress of grass-green velvet with gold frogs. Her green velvet hat, high-crowned and with a curled brim, was tipped over her black curls at a rakish angle.

Several gentlemen tried to accost her, and, at last, Yvonne went in to the most fashionable-looking shop she could see to avoid them.

The shopkeeper was very helpful. To her inquiries he replied that there was a Corby Hall at the west end of the town, but a family called Battersby from Yorkshire had been living there for the past twenty years.

Yvonne, determined to have exact proof of Patricia's lying, was just asking him directions to Corby Hall so that she might question the Battersbys herself — after all, they might have had relatives called Paxton living with them — when the shopkeeper exclaimed, "Why, if it isn't Mrs. Battersby herself!"

A lady who looked, thought Yvonne, like a particularly mondaine ferret advanced on them. She had reddish eyes and a long thin nose and very sharp teeth.

"If you please, madam," said Yvonne with a very low curtsy, "I am Lady de la Falaise. I am checking the references of my governess, Miss Cottingham, who claims to have been employed by a Mrs. Paxton of Corby Hall."

"French!" exclaimed Mrs. Battersby, drawing back her skirts. "This country is riddled with

French spies. Paxton, indeed. That for a tale. Never heard of them or this Miss Cottingham. Get along with you, you — you *frog eater*."

"Your manners, madam," said Yvonne, her cheeks flaming, "are as bad as your appearance. Good day to you!"

She marched to the door of the shop, her head held high.

As she gained the street, Mrs. Battersby stuck her head around the shop door and shouted after her, "We don't need no Frenchies here!"

People turned to stare at Yvonne. She felt ready to sink through the pavement with embarrassment. But she had achieved her object. Patricia had lied about the Truro reference and no doubt had forged the other one as well.

With a sigh of relief, she turned in at the doorway of the Three Feathers. Soon she would be on her way, and with any luck the viscount, finding her horse gone from the stables, would have assumed she had gone out riding for the day.

But disaster stared her in the face when she opened the door of the taproom. Her coachman lay slumped in the corner, dead drunk.

Although Yvonne's accent was now very light, it was unmistakably French, and when the men in the tap heard her exclaim, "*Parbleu!* What am I to do now? How did he become drunk so quickly?" there was a hostile murmur.

"Where d'ye come from, Frenchie?" growled

a beefy-looking man. "Looking for frogs to eat?"

"I am not called Frenchie," said Yvonne haughtily. "My name is Lady de la Falaise."

"So *you* says," growled another voice. "That's what they all says. Every Frenchie's an aristocrat that comes here. Struttin' about with their foreign ways, takin' bread out o' the mouths o' good Englishmen."

Yvonne retreated quickly. It was useless to stand in a common tap listening to insults. She would need to find another carriage.

But on hearing her accent, the two livery stables in the town refused to hire her a carriage. England was at war with France. Yvonne was French. She was the enemy. Had she explained she was the ward of Lord Anselm of Trewent Castle, all animosity would have faded, but Yvonne, who was used to being treated with respect by the castle servants, was too bewildered to think clearly and did not realize the hatred for the French that gripped England.

Insults were beginning to be shouted at her in the streets as the news of her nationality spread. Yvonne thought quickly. It was only a matter of three leagues to Penryn. She would walk.

Once clear of the town, she heaved a sigh of relief. A good steady pace for a few hours would take her to Penryn. At least she was moving faster on her own two feet than she had done when riding in the antiquated carriage.

A heavy drop of rain struck her cheek. She looked up. The sky was purple-black. On the horizon a fork of lightning stabbed down, and there came the menacing rumble of thunder.

Yvonne quickened her pace.

Viscount Anselm rode out before the rising storm, his face as black with anger as the storm clouds piling up on the horizon.

When Patricia had told him that Yvonne had not put in an appearance at her lessons, he had assumed she had gone out riding. He would have gone on assuming this had not the carrier from Penryn arrived with a parcel of books and told the interested servants that a French lady who was said to be Lord Anselm's ward had arrived in Penryn on horseback, had stabled her horse, and had hired Tom Bodkin and his broken-down old carriage to take her to Truro. Bets were being laid in the town as to whether Tom — a notorious drunk — would ever make it.

This fascinating piece of intelligence was duly communicated to his lordship by the butler, Fairbairn. Gustave Bouvet was sent for but disclaimed all knowledge of his mistress's whereabouts, adding coldly that he would never have allowed her to ride out alone.

The viscount was about to send for Patricia when he suddenly remembered Yvonne's curiosity about Patricia's references. He took both of them from the desk and studied them. One, he noted, came from Truro.

All at once he became convinced Yvonne had set out to check Patricia's Truro reference. He decided to go after her himself. He would not tell Patricia. Her charge's hurtful, suspicious behavior must be kept from her.

He found Yvonne's horse stabled at Penryn and then rode off once more in the direction of Truro, the rising wind lifting his black cloak from his shoulders and sending it streaming out behind him.

The storm finally broke over his head. Blinding sheets of rain swept over the moors. Thunder rumbled and rolled, and hellish flashes of lightning pierced the nightmare scene.

By the light of one of these flashes he saw a solitary little figure trudging along the road toward him.

He reined in his horse and glared down at Yvonne de la Falaise. Her riding hat was a soaking ruin, and her velvet riding dress was plastered to her body.

He held his hand out. "Up," he commanded.

Yvonne swung lightly up behind him. He could feel her body trembling with cold, and she kept saying over and over again, "I am so sorry."

"Save your apologies until I find us some shelter," he shouted over his shoulder. He spurred his horse toward Truro.

As they reached the outskirts of the town, the

clouds rolled away and the sun shone down on a wet and glittering world.

The viscount rode straight to the George, Truro's biggest posting house. He dismounted and lifted Yvonne down, barked at her, "Follow me," and strode into the inn.

Viscount Anselm was immediately recognized. Despite the fact that his lordship was muddy and wet and had a disaster of a female with him, the landlord appeared bowing his nose down to the ground and offering every kind of service and help.

Yvonne was handed over to two housemaids and hustled up to a bedchamber. Her wet clothes were removed, and she was dressed in a clean nightgown and wrapped in a quilt and told to sit beside the fire until clothes were found for her.

The maids were soon back with bundles of clothes. The landlord's servants had run hither and thither requesting dry clothes for Lord Anselm's ward. It seemed every genteel female in the town who heard of Yvonne's predicament wanted a chance to find favor in the handsome viscount's eyes. The landlord's wife selected what she thought was the best and sent the rest back. She was quite puffed up with the importance of caring for the viscount's ward, declaring Yvonne to be the prettiest miss you ever did see and quite forgetting she had been jeering at Yvonne in the street earlier in the day.

Such was the viscount's importance in the area that all Yvonne's Frenchness disappeared from the eyes of the townspeople.

Yvonne received a curt message from her guardian saying they would need to stay the night, as the roads were too bad to travel. She was to present herself at the dinner table at five o'clock.

Yvonne worked hard on her appearance. She selected a pretty pink muslin gown that tied under the bosom with long satin ribbons. Since she was still feeling cold, she draped a fine Paisley shawl about her shoulders and arranged her now dry and shining hair in the most modish of Grecian styles.

She did not feel in the slightest ashamed of her behavior. Lord Anselm should learn how that paragon of a governess had tricked him.

And she would be alone with her guardian. No Patricia to take his attention away from her.

Her heart beating hard with excitement, she pushed open the door of the private parlor where the landlord's wife had told her dinner was to be served — and then stood on the threshold, struggling to hide her dismay.

For her guardian was not alone. With him at the table was a prosperous-looking couple. The gentleman was fat and rubicund, and his wife was small and faded.

"My ward, Yvonne, Lady de la Falaise," said the viscount, rising to his feet. "Yvonne, may I have the honor of presenting my friends, Mr.

and Mrs. Leamon. They are residents of Truro, and Mr. Leamon, on hearing of my predicament, found dry clothes for me. They have graciously accepted my invitation to dinner."

The viscount frowned at Mr. Leamon, who was goggling at Yvonne.

Yvonne shook hands with them both. The viscount pulled out a chair for her, and she sat down at the table.

"*Est-ce-que* that *vous* likez notter payee?" asked Mrs. Leamon suddenly.

The viscount saw Yvonne's startled look and translated Mrs. Leamon's bad French. "Mrs. Leamon is asking whether you like our country," he said.

"Very much," replied Yvonne demurely, casting a glance at Mr. Leamon from under her long lashes. She knew Mr. Leamon was much taken with her and hoped the viscount noticed.

The viscount *had* noticed his friend's thunderstruck admiration and was extremely irritated by it. Tommy Leamon was the same age as he was himself and ought to be above goggling at pretty misses in their teens, thought the viscount sourly.

He would not admit to himself that he had been taken aback by Yvonne's great beauty when she had first entered the room. It struck him like a hammer blow that she was not the child he had imagined her to be but a highly desirable woman. She had none of the gauche manners of an English miss of the same age.

Mrs. Leamon tried again to speak to Yvonne in broken French and looked very disappointed when Yvonne said politely that she spoke English very well, so there was no reason to try to address her in French.

"I was not *trying*," said Mrs. Leamon rather huffily. "All my friends say I speak French like a native."

The viscount thought Yvonne murmured "of the South Seas," but she returned his suspicious look with a limpid gaze.

During that long and tedious dinner, the viscount could only admire his ward's tact and behavior. Although he had known Tommy Leamon and his wife for some years, their company in the past had always been diluted with other people, and therefore it had not been brought to his attention before that both were colossal bores.

Yvonne surprised him by smiling charmingly and saying little. At one point she gave a little start and looked rather reproachfully at Mr. Leamon and said, "I fear the space under the table must be a trifle cramped, Mr. Leamon, for you have pressed my foot by *accident* several times."

It was then that the viscount realized he was tired. His ward needed an early night, he said, and the port was quite dreadful, so Tommy would no doubt forgive them.

Mr. Leamon and his wife reluctantly took their leave.

"Now, Yvonne," said the viscount grimly, "it is time we had a talk."

"I find it incredible you can actually bring yourself to talk to me without the presence of a chaperone," said Yvonne. "Besides, you chased the Leamons away saying the port was too dreadful to drink and yet you are pouring it out." She gave him a mocking look, but the viscount would not be drawn into criticizing his friends.

"I want to get to the bottom of this," he said. "I understand that your jealousy of Patricia Cottingham — that sterling lady who has twice saved your life — drove you to check the validity of the Truro reference."

"Intelligent suspicion drove me," said Yvonne. "And I was right! The reference is false."

"You are sure?"

"Yes. The lady who lives at Corby Hall is a Yorkshire woman of most unpleasant manners. She delighted in telling me that no Paxton had ever lived there, and Paxton is the name on the reference."

"I refuse to believe ill of Miss Cottingham," said the viscount half to himself. He twirled his glass and sent a little wave of port up the sides. "No doubt there will be some explanation."

"Oh, yes," said Yvonne, looking at him in dawning dismay. "There will!"

"Explain yourself!"

Yvonne turned a clear gaze on her guardian. In a startling imitation of Patricia's voice, she said, "I was driven to lie, my lord. Please forgive me. You, who have so much, do not know what it is to be poor and friendless. I had never had to work before. What I told you about my family, *that* was true, but, alas, how could I obtain a good post without references? Have I done anything to show myself unworthy of that post? And you will say —"

"Enough, you wretched little actress," snapped the viscount. "How did you know she had told me of her family and that they were poor?"

"It stands to reason that they must have been, or are in straitened circumstances, or she would never have had to work," pointed out Yvonne, "and any employer would ask about family and background."

"If she does ask me whether she has done anything to show herself unworthy of her post," said the viscount, "then I shall be forced to tell her the truth — to admit she is a lady I am *proud* to have in my home."

"And in your heart?"

"What do you know of hearts — you, who are barely out of the schoolroom?"

"You are so English." Yvonne sighed. "And yet your friend Mr. Leamon did not see me as a little girl. Neither will many men. He pressed my foot so warmly. . . ."

"I cannot believe any man would do such a thing with his wife present. You made a mistake."

"Pooh, fiddlesticks, and fustian!"

"Furthermore, to ride off on your own to Penryn, to hire a broken-down carriage and a drunken driver to go in search of ammunition to fire at your poor governess was not the action of a mature woman. Had Miss Cottingham been cruel to you or neglectful of her duties, then I might have understood it. As it is, you have caused me discomfort and embarrassment —"

"Since you obviously find the care of me so weighty," interrupted Yvonne, "perhaps you should be looking out for a suitable gentleman for me."

"I do not know any gentleman who would beat you as you deserve."

"La! How fierce you are! Do you advocate wife-beating?"

"In your case, yes."

"You are drinking a great deal of wine. It is the port that is beginning to talk."

"I can hold my wine very well, miss. But you may have the right of it — I should be looking for a husband for you. Perhaps I might give a ball. It is time I entertained the local county."

"But where? There is no ballroom in the castle."

"If the weather is fine, we can erect marquees on the lawns. If not, that chain of dreary saloons and drawing rooms on the first floor will suffice. They will need to be decorated."

Yvonne clasped her hands, her large eyes

sparkling. "I can see it now . . . all the grand people of the county. . . ."

"And many not so grand. At a country ball, one has to invite everyone from the village as well."

"I have a beautiful ball gown," said Yvonne, "but no jewelry."

"There are the Anselm diamonds."

"Which I shall wear!" cried Yvonne.

"Which you have no right to wear. Traditionally, they will be worn only by my wife."

"But you have no wife and so —"

"And so they will stay right where they are until I do have one. It is not fashionable in this country for young unmarried misses to deck themselves out like a shop window."

"Pooh!" said Yvonne. "If I listen to you much longer, I shall begin to believe it is not fashionable to have any fun at all. I *like* wearing pretty things. I like flirting."

"Nonsense. You cannot have had much experience of flirting at your age."

Yvonne looked amused. "I was very strictly chaperoned. But there was always church on Sundays. The little glance, the dropped handkerchief, the sighs, the secret notes —"

"Enough! I think you had better go to bed or you might demoralize me completely."

Yvonne rose to her feet and he pushed back his chair and got up at the same time, looking down at her from his great height.

"I shall kiss you good night, my stern

guardian," said Yvonne.

She looked so young and so very pretty that he smiled and offered his cheek. "Very well," he said.

Yvonne stood on tiptoe, wound her arms tightly about his neck, and kissed him full on the mouth.

He felt his senses reeling; he felt such an aching surge of passion that for one delirious moment he forgot he held his ward in his arms. Then he pushed her roughly away and moved behind his chair, hanging on to the back and breathing heavily.

"Get out of here, you *jade*," he grated.

Yvonne kissed the tips of her fingers to him and tripped from the room.

But once she had closed the door behind her, she leaned her back against it and prayed he would call her back. But there was nothing but silence from inside the parlor.

With a disappointed little sigh, she went slowly along to her room.

The viscount sat down abruptly as if his legs had given way.

The sooner Yvonne de La Falaise was married, the better!

Chapter Six

Yvonne should have fallen asleep immediately, exhausted as she was from her long walk. But she had forgotten to draw the curtains at the window or the curtains around her bed, and bright moonlight flooded the room.

She twisted and turned restlessly against the pillows, longing to hear the rumble of thunder. Another storm would mean the roads would still be too bad on the morrow for them to journey home. That way she would have her guardian all to herself for one more precious day.

"I shall never sleep unless I pull the curtains," she murmured, climbing down from the high bed. But instead of drawing the curtains, she opened the window and looked out. The air was sweet and cool, and moonlight flooded the inn courtyard.

Yvonne twisted her neck and looked up at the sky. Not a cloud in sight. She was about to close the window again when she saw a tall figure glide across the entrance to the courtyard.

There was something in the graceful move-ment, something in the turn of the head that made Yvonne catch her breath and exclaim, "Patricia!"

As she watched, the woman she was sure was Patricia was joined by two darker, squatter fig-ures, both men. Patricia, if it was she, said something, and then three faces, white disks in the moonlight, turned and looked at the inn.

Yvonne drew back, suddenly afraid. She ran from her room to that of her guardian, which was next door, and plunged on top of his sleeping figure, shaking him by his naked shoulders to wake him.

The rush light beside the bed, burning in its pierced cannister, revealed to the viscount that his ward was wearing an even more frivolous nightgown than the one he had seen her wearing before.

"I am afraid," said Yvonne, her accent be-coming more markedly French in her agitation. "The governess — Patricia — she is watching the inn."

"Fustian."

Yvonne crawled forward on the bed and tugged at his hand. "No! I speak the truth. Come. I will show you."

The viscount jerked his hand free and then pulled the blankets, which had slid to his waist, up about his neck and stared angrily at his ward, who retreated to the foot of the bed.

"If this is one of your games . . . Turn your

back, girl, while I find my dressing gown."

Yvonne did not turn her back. Instead, she covered her eyes with her hands until he told her curtly that he had put on his dressing gown.

"Now, show me," he commanded.

Yvonne opened the window. He pressed close behind her, and she could feel the warmth of his body through the thin cambric of her nightgown.

The yard was empty. Bright moonlight silvered the cobbles.

"Well?" he demanded. "Are you sure you are not beginning to *imagine* Patricia's villainy on every occasion?"

Yvonne was shaken, shaken as much by his physical nearness as by the fear she *had* been imagining that tall figure in the courtyard.

"I did see her . . . or someone who looked very like her," she insisted.

The viscount sighed impatiently. "Go to bed, Yvonne," he said. "And next time something frightens you, do not come bursting into my bedchamber. I have no wish to be compromised."

"You! Compromised!" Yvonne gasped with outrage. "Let me tell you I would not marry you were you the last man on earth."

"Trite, but possibly true," he said equably. "Nonetheless, had any member of the local county seen you entering my bedchamber, then I would most certainly have had to marry you."

Yvonne could hardly understand her own great hurt, her own sharp and bitter feeling of rejection. He had returned her kiss. She had not imagined *that!*

Did he not realize all she wanted from him was recognition and attention, not to be treated as one of his servants or dependents?

"Good night, my lord," she said stiffly. "I shall not trouble you again."

"Oh, I am sure you shall," he said bitterly. "Trouble is your name, Yvonne de la Falaise."

She pushed past him, wrenching open the door of his room and slamming it behind her with enough force to bring a volley of oaths from the other guests at the inn resounding along the corridor.

It was a silent journey back to the castle the next morning. The earl had hired a carriage and was driving it himself, sitting up on the box with Yvonne beside him.

The nightmarish weather of the day before might never have happened. The landscape smiled under a warm sun, and a thin mist gave the stunted moorland trees and the small round moorland hills the beauty of a Chinese painting.

Yvonne glanced sideways at the viscount's stern face. He was still wearing the ill-fitting clothes his friend Mr. Leamon had found for him. But he still managed to look elegant and beautiful. It was odd to think of a man being beautiful, reflected Yvonne, but the viscount's sculptured, classical features reminded her of a Greek god.

She comforted herself by telling herself severely that he was autocratic and overbearing and had not one ounce of sensibility in his whole body. His body! As the team of horses raced along the bumpy road, the viscount braced his feet against the splashboard, and she could see the long line of muscle rippling along his thighs, which were encased in tight leather breeches. Yvonne blushed and turned her head away. The viscount was beginning to disturb her physically, and her body did not feel like her own. It refused to obey the stern lectures it was receiving from her brain and leaned toward him like a plant toward the sun with every jolt and sway of the carriage.

The viscount was a very worried man. He had never reacted in the whole of his life to any woman's kiss the way he had reacted to the one given him by Yvonne de la Falaise.

It was all the fault of a long period of celibacy, combined with his increasing years, he thought gloomily. Imagine a man beginning to lust after his own ward, and she barely out of the schoolroom!

He longed to escape back into the routine of the castle life, where competent Patricia would once again take over the education of Yvonne.

As the ugly bulk of Trewent Castle loomed into view, Yvonne broke into speech. "Why is it you live in such a horrible place?"

"You have been mercifully silent for the past few hours," snapped the viscount. "Please continue to remain so."

Gustave was waiting in the courtyard to berate his mistress. Yvonne, not knowing the viscount understood French very well — after all, explaining Mrs. Leamon's broken French had only required a smattering of the language combined with common sense — answered back, her face blazing with fury.

With all the familiarity of an old servant, Gustave was accusing Yvonne of extreme folly in riding off without him, blaming her for an overactive imagination. Yvonne tore back at him, telling him he would surely have lost his job at the castle had he been found to have aided her.

The earl at last interrupted this interesting scene by curtly ordering Gustave back to the stables and commanding Yvonne to follow him into the castle.

He asked Fairbairn to tell Miss Cottingham to attend them in the library.

"Now we shall see," he said grimly. He went to the desk and took out Patricia's references and laid them on a table in front of him.

Patricia came in, immediately voicing her concern over Yvonne's disappearance from the castle and her relief that all was now well. Then her eye fell on the two references and then rose to survey the viscount's stony face and her voice faltered into silence.

"One of your references, Miss Cottingham," said the viscount, "states you were employed by a Mrs. Paxton of Truro. It has been brought to my attention there is no such person."

Patricia glanced sadly and reproachfully at Yvonne before turning away to look out of the window.

"I lied, my lord," she said. "I confess I lied. But I was left penniless. I had to find work. You would not have employed me without references."

She swung around and faced the viscount, tears glittering in her eyes. Yvonne caught her breath. Patricia looked like a tragic heroine. Her face was pale, and the tears in her eyes enhanced their brilliance.

Patricia spread her hands in a pathetic pleading movement. "I know it is hard for you, my lord, to understand how poor and desperate I was. But have I done anything since my arrival to show myself unworthy of the post?"

Her hands fell limply to her sides as she looked at the viscount's bleak face. "Ah, I see it is of no use. Never fear. I shall leave without fuss."

"No," said the viscount, although his expression did not change. "I shall dismiss you only when I find you cannot do the job for which you were engaged. We will say no more about this matter. Do not lie to me again."

Patricia dropped gracefully to her knees and

knelt before him. She raised tear-washed eyes to his face in humble gratitude.

"Oh, my lord," she whispered, "how can I ever thank you?"

The viscount's face softened as he looked down at her.

"Please rise, Miss Cottingham," he said gently. "The matter is at an end. Go about your duties."

Patricia rose, murmuring her thanks, and quietly left the room.

As the door closed behind her, Yvonne applauded softly. "Bravo!" she said.

"Are you applauding me or Miss Cottingham?" demanded the viscount.

"Why, Miss Cottingham, of course. What a performance! I confess she nearly had me in tears. Who would have thought that such a Siddons could blossom in this rural backwater!"

"You force me to remind you that that lady has been twice — *twice* — responsible for saving your life."

"As to that," said Yvonne, leaning forward, "I have a theory. . . ."

The viscount looked at her, appalled. "So now you are going to say she did not really rescue you. It was the Cornish fairies after all. Oh, go away, Yvonne. You weary me."

"Bad cess to you, you bad-mannered lout," raged Yvonne, cut to the quick. "I *told* you what she would say, and she *did*. But nothing will change your stupid mind about your precious Miss Cottingham, you . . . you great oaf!"

She flew at him in a passion as he rose to his feet. In a black rage, he slapped her across the face. It was a light slap with no force behind it. Yvonne stood stock-still, her face as white as paper. The viscount looked at his own hand as if he could not believe his eyes.

"I am sorry," he said, looking at her in amazement. "But you drive me mad."

"Oh, my lord," said Yvonne, imitating Patricia's voice to perfection. "How can I ever thank you?" She strode to the door and then looked back at him, her black eyes snapping. "Do not worry, my *dear* guardian. I shall most certainly think of something."

After she had left, the viscount sank into a chair and, seizing his golden curls, tugged his hair hard. "What on earth came over me?" he wondered. All of his female charges had, in the past, proved to be more infuriating in their behavior than Yvonne. But he would never have struck any of them. Never!

He would need to apologize sincerely and humbly to Yvonne. But she *asked* for it, he told himself savagely. He had hoped, he realized, that all his old respect and admiration for Patricia would have been rekindled when he saw her again, would have driven out the increasing attraction Yvonne was beginning to hold for him. And it would have been reanimated, he thought, had not Yvonne so cleverly anticipated how Patricia would behave and what she would say.

Not that that made Miss Cottingham a schemer or an untrustworthy woman. The viscount trusted his own instincts. No woman of such bravery, such ladylike bearing as Patricia Cottingham, could be capable of treachery or deceit. It was understandable that any gentlewoman in her circumstances would be forced to forge references in order to obtain a post.

Yvonne must be married as soon as possible and Patricia pensioned off.

Then he would *shoot* any female who dared to approach the castle, who dared to threaten the peace of his bachelor life.

In the weeks that followed, Patricia and Yvonne managed surprisingly well. It was as if both women had privately agreed on some sort of truce. Neither made any reference to Patricia's lies or Yvonne's visit to Truro.

But Yvonne was still secretly determined to find out if Patricia was really as brave as she had appeared to be on both occasions when she had rescued her.

Yvonne had accepted the viscount's apology with outer grace and inner disappointment. For the viscount had been grave and kind, and she would rather have had him storm at her, shake her, show that she sparked *some* emotion in him.

Yvonne now received a generous allowance

from the viscount. She had wanted to buy ribbons to embellish a gown, and when she had asked him for the money, he had realized he had never thought of providing her with pin money.

Yvonne was still furious with Gustave for upbraiding her in front of the viscount, and so she kept her speculations about Patricia to herself.

The castle was a restless place, full of painters and builders and men hanging new curtains. Yvonne found only a little satisfaction in noticing that the viscount did not appear to have consulted Patricia about decoration or design.

But he still saw the governess at four o'clock most afternoons. Yvonne wondered what they talked about, but she did not want to be caught eavesdropping again.

Besides, it was becoming harder to imagine sinister motives seething behind Patricia's placid brow as one lazy golden summer day followed another. Suspicion was no longer fueled by jealousy, because Yvonne never saw the viscount and Patricia together.

Yvonne began to visit the village of Trewent fairly often, taking Gustave with her and leaving him at a local inn while she went down to the small harbor to watch the fishing boats.

Suspicions belonged to the winter nights, the dark days, and the rainy days. Yvonne would have abandoned any plans to test Patricia's bravery, had not a strange sight brought all her doubts flooding back.

She was riding back to the castle from the village one afternoon with Gustave at her side. She reined in at the top of the cliff path and said to her servant, "I wonder if they have a new boat."

"It looks dangerous," growled Gustave. "Don't go down there, milady."

"You have become an old woman, Gustave," said Yvonne crossly. "Guard the horses. I shall return in a moment."

She had been gone fifteen minutes, and Gustave was just debating whether to tether the horses and follow his mistress when Yvonne reappeared, much flushed.

"It's back, Gustave," she cried. "The boat, the *Trewent Castle*, is tied to the jetty."

"The thieves probably returned it," said Gustave indifferently. "Keeping such a boat would identify them."

"Well, I think it most odd," said Yvonne impatiently. "They could have burned it or disguised it — but to risk capture by returning it!"

"Milady," said Gustave patiently, "do not make the mysteries. So Miss Cottingham lied about a reference. So now everything is suspicious. Me, I would do the same thing, should the need arise."

Yvonne thought furiously on the road back. She must see her guardian immediately.

Her heart gave a queer little jerk when she saw the viscount striding toward the castle from the stables. He was hatless and wearing only a fine cambric shirt, leather breeches, and top boots. He walked with easy, athletic grace, and his fair hair was ruffled by the gentle breeze.

"My lord!" called Yvonne, her voice made sharp with irritation. For he had shown every sign of walking on without staying to greet her.

He swung about and stood with his hands on his hips, watching her dismount. She was wearing an alpaca riding dress of mannish cut. Her long skirt caught on one of the stirrups, exposing a flurry of white lace petticoat.

He had not seen her for some time, having carefully kept away from her. Now he wondered again how he could ever have considered her a little girl. It was a seductive woman with skin tanned to pale gold and a swelling bosom above a tiny waist who came tripping toward him.

"What is it, Yvonne?" he asked.

"The boat, the *Trewent Castle* — it's back," cried Yvonne.

A smile crossed the viscount's face as he looked beyond her. Yvonne whipped around, her skirts belling out about her slim body. Gustave was piously rolling his eyes up to the sky in mock resignation.

"Go to the stables, Gustave," snapped Yvonne. "I shall deal with you later."

"Quietly, my termagant," said the viscount. "The rowing boat was returned a day after your capture."

"And you did not find that odd?" exclaimed Yvonne.

Unconsciously repeating Gustave's argument, the viscount said, "No doubt they were frightened that possession of the boat would lead us to them."

"Fiddlesticks! Thieves are thieves, and a good boat is a good boat. *Tiens!* They could have sold it or painted it or burned it."

The viscount threw her a mocking look. "Next you will be accusing your poor governess of having spirited it back into place."

"That would not surprise me in the least," said Yvonne.

"It is back, and there have been no more signs of the brigands." The viscount sighed, evidently becoming bored with the subject. "The ball is in a week's time. You are expected to stand at my side and greet my guests. Remember to be on your best behavior. You are protected from anti-French feeling by my patronage. Do not do or say anything to give the local worthies a disgust of you."

"I am always convenable," said Yvonne with a toss of her curls.

"See that you continue to be so. What is it, Fairbairn?" The butler had approached quietly while they were talking.

"Miss Cottingham awaits you in the library, my lord."

"Four o'clock already! Good-bye, Yvonne."

The viscount turned on his heel and strode into the castle.

Yvonne watched him go, her hands clenched at her sides. Green-eyed jealousy came roaring back and, with it, stronger and deeper suspicions about Patricia's character. He conversed with Patricia each time for only about five or ten minutes. But that was enough, thought Yvonne, to strengthen the intimacy.

All her determination not to eavesdrop left her. She darted around to the castle to the front and crept quietly up the steps to the narrow terrace that ran along the front of the building. The library window was open.

Frightened to look in through the window in case she might be seen, Yvonne listened hard.

"I would like to see my ward spend more of her outings in your company," she heard the viscount say.

"I fear she prefers the company of her French groom," Patricia replied.

"He is a sterling fellow, but she converses with him in French, and it is important that she should begin to consider herself an English-woman. Be careful not to go near Penryn, however. There are two dangerous footpads on the loose, and they have not yet been apprehended."

"Very good, my lord."

There was a little silence, a rustle of papers, and then the viscount said, "That will be all for today, Miss Cottingham."

Yvonne heaved a sigh of relief. All very formal. The viscount was speaking very much as employer to employed.

Then she heard Patricia say, "Am I invited to your ball, my lord?"

"Of course."

Patricia's voice held that teasing, flirtatious note that Yvonne had heard once before. "I shall sit with the chaperones, my lord, and watch the dancing. Should I wear a cap?"

"You may dance, Miss Cottingham. All of the local people are to attend. We do not stand on ceremony at a country ball."

"At least I cannot expect a dance from *you,* my lord. *That* would occasion too much comment, even at a country ball."

"I would be honored if you would favor me with a dance, Miss Cottingham," said the viscount stiffly.

What else *could* he say? thought Yvonne, grinding her teeth.

"And pray make sure my high-spirited ward behaves herself," she heard the viscount add.

"Yes, that is most important," Patricia replied seriously. "Particularly with so much anti-French feeling in England. It is a pity Yvonne is not English. The French are so emotional, so unstable, so much given to wild flights of fancy."

The viscount replied something, but as, Yvonne judged, he had crossed the room to hold open the door for Patricia, she could not hear what he said.

Yvonne was in a thoroughly bad temper. Patricia should learn the French were a match for the English. The governess seemed to have iced water in her veins. "Let her find herself in a situation of apparently real danger, and then we shall see how genuine that famous English calm of hers really is!" vowed Yvonne.

It was a mile and a half to the village. Yvonne set out on foot.

She did not want even Gustave to know what she planned to do.

Chapter Seven

Perhaps hoping to save the governess from having to argue with his tempestuous ward, the viscount summoned Yvonne the next morning and told her that he expected her to take Miss Cottingham along with her when she went out that afternoon.

To his surprise, Yvonne readily agreed, and surprised him further by asking if she might take out a small gig she had seen in the stables.

Cautiously, the viscount agreed, but only after having had a horse harnessed to the gig and having seen Yvonne demonstrate to a nicety that she could drive a light carriage as easily as she could ride.

Patricia was obviously relieved she was not expected to ride, and at three in the afternoon both ladies set out in the gig, taking a little-used road across the moors.

Yvonne was in high good humor, laughing and singing French songs. Yvonne knew that once they were away from the castle, they would be set upon by two footpads. For had she not arranged the whole thing herself?

The evening before, she had found two sturdy young men in the village who had readily agreed to act the part of footpads. Their instructions were to frighten the governess but not harm her. They were to find a boy to run to the castle with the news of the "attack" so that, with luck, Lord Anselm would arrive in time to witness Yvonne's bravery but not in good enough time to stop the "footpads" from escaping. One of the young men said his brother would act as messenger.

Yvonne held the reins in one hand and surreptitiously felt the hard bulk that was the pistol inside her reticule.

As usual, Patricia was talking of everything and nothing. Yvonne reflected, not for the first time, that it was amazing how the governess could talk so much without ever betraying anything about herself. She talked of the material she had found in Penryn to make herself a gown for the ball, of the pleasant summer weather, of the poor quality of mutton from the sheep grazing on the moors, and of the new decorating of the castle, agreeing with Yvonne that not much in the way of flowers or hangings could really do much to alleviate the gloom of the place.

And then two men rose up from the heather, brandishing cudgels. Even Yvonne, who had been expecting them, let out a scream.

For the young men from Trewent were surely masters in the art of disguise. They made a villainous-looking pair, reflected Yvonne, stunned with admiration.

One of the men had seized the reins of the startled and plunging horse. "Get down," he growled, "or it will be the worse for you."

Patricia, white to the lips, started to get down. But to Yvonne's disappointment, she showed no signs of screaming or fainting. Yvonne gently drew her little pistol out of her reticule. "And you," the other man shouted at her.

As Yvonne was getting down, Patricia whipped about and started to run. "Help!" she screamed. "Help me!"

As Yvonne watched, stricken, one of the men ran after Patricia, raised his cudgel, and brought the governess down with a heavy blow on the head.

"You're not supposed to do that," gasped Yvonne. "Have you both gone mad?"

The one who had stayed to guard Yvonne and the carriage shouted to his friend, "See if she's got any money on her."

"If she ain't, she's got something nearly as good," called back the man, stooping over Patricia.

As Yvonne watched with dilated eyes, the ruffian turned Patricia's unconscious body over with his foot, and one dirty hand started fumbling inside the neck of the governess's muslin gown.

Yvonne stared at the man next to her, at the

low brow, filthy face, and red-rimmed eyes. In that one panic-stricken moment, she realized they were not the young men she had hired, but genuine footpads.

"Now you," said her guard, grinning at her and raising his cudgel. "Let's see what you got."

Yvonne raised her pistol, which had been hidden in the folds of her skirt.

"Come and 'elp me, Jem," called her guard. "She got a gun."

"Take it from her, man," yelled his companion. "She won't know how to use it."

Yvonne lowered the pistol until it was pointing at the man's leg. He made a sudden grab, but she fired first.

He let out a scream of pain, wailing, "I been hit."

His companion started to run away just as the thud of hooves came along the road from the direction of the castle.

Yvonne recklessly ran after him, shouting for help as the figure of the viscount, riding hell for leather, appeared on the crest of the road.

He rode straight for the escaping man and brought the butt end of his whip down on the ruffian's head, knocking him unconscious. A little way behind him came some of the castle servants, headed by Gustave.

The viscount dismounted and kicked the body of the man he had stunned. "Tie this one up," he called, "and catch that other one."

The man Yvonne had shot was trying to limp across the moor.

The viscount waited until he saw both men were being dealt with, then he turned silently to Yvonne and held out his arms.

She flung herself into them, hugging him tightly, pressing her face close against his chest and hearing the erratic thumping of his heart.

A faint moan came from somewhere nearby. "Miss Cottingham," cried the viscount, pushing Yvonne away.

He ran forward and knelt on the ground beside the governess. "I am not going to let him take her in his arms," vowed Yvonne.

She ran forward and knelt down as well. "I will attend her," she said. "My poor Patricia. She had such a fright, my lord. She was hit by one of those men when she was running away."

"And did you not try to run as well?" demanded the viscount, smoothing Patricia's hair back from her brow. It was all Yvonne could do to stop herself from snatching his hand away.

"I shot mine," she said.

The viscount sat back on his heels and stared at her in amazement. "You shot him! What with?"

"My pistol," said Yvonne, holding it out. "Patricia had no reason to be so very frightened. *I* would have looked after her."

Yvonne shivered slightly with shock and with a sudden feeling of self-disgust. She, Yvonne, was behaving abominably. Patricia might have been killed. She had proved to be almost as courageous as she had done before.

But then the viscount said, "We shall talk more of this later," and he leaned forward and started to slide his arm under Patricia's shoulders to lift her up.

Jealousy, sharp as a knife wound, stabbed at Yvonne's breast and she said, "No!" And then in a milder voice, "No. You must let me take care of my dear governess. Gustave! Come here and lift Miss Cottingham into the carriage. You, my lord, should make sure both men are tied up securely."

Patricia regained consciousness. Her blue eyes looked long and steadily up into Yvonne's black ones as Lord Anselm released her and walked off.

"I . . . do . . . not . . . believe . . . those . . . men . . . were . . . real . . . footpads," choked Patricia in a hoarse whisper.

Yvonne's black eyes narrowed. "And why should you think that, *dear* Patricia?" she hissed.

Gustave came up and lifted Patricia in his arms. Yvonne followed them to the carriage. The full shock of the whole episode now hit her. Her knees wobbled and her eyes filled with tears. She longed to throw herself back into the viscount's arms and cry her eyes out. But he must see how brave she was. He must! So Yvonne climbed into the carriage and sat with her back rigid, staring straight ahead while Gustave helped Patricia into the gig. Yvonne did not know that the viscount had noticed Yvonne's eyes, bright with unshed tears, had noticed the faint trembling of her hands, and was overcome by a wave of tenderness that no stoic bravery could have roused in his bosom.

Patricia was put to bed as soon as they reached the castle. Yvonne sat beside her until the sleeping draught that the governess had been given began to take effect.

But before Patricia's eyes closed, Yvonne leaned over her and said, "You must know now that the footpads were real, Patricia. They have been taken off to prison in Penryn under armed guard. What made you think otherwise?"

Patricia's blue eyes looked sleepy and puzzled. "I do not know what it is you are trying to say."

"When you recovered consciousness," said Yvonne, "you said the men were not real footpads. What did you mean?"

She waited eagerly for the governess's reply. If it turned out that Patricia had heard gossip from the village that two young men had been paid to act as footpads, then it would follow that she had every reason to believe the attack a vicious trick.

But Patricia's clear gaze only registered surprise. She put a hand to her head. "I cannot recall saying any such thing, Yvonne," said Patricia. "We were both shocked, and the mind can play strange tricks. Please leave me."

Her eyes closed.

Yvonne slipped quietly from her room and went to her own sitting room and sat looking out at the sea, thinking hard.

Patricia *had* said those words. Why should she think the whole attack a charade unless . . . unless she herself had been guilty of organizing such a sham attack.

She went in search of her guardian, only to find that he had gone into Penryn with the armed guard. She wandered off to the stables and told Gustave to make ready to accompany her to the village.

But Gustave said roundly he would do no such thing. Her ladyship should be in bed after the shocks of the day. He himself would not move an inch from the castle grounds unless it was with the permission of Lord Anselm.

He glared suspiciously at his mistress when she meekly accepted his rebellion and watched her with narrowed eyes as she went back into the castle.

Yvonne went straight into the library and climbed out through the open window and then made her way on foot toward the village of Trewent.

The sun was setting by the time she reached the village, and she was hot and cross and suffering from reaction to the fright she had received.

As she walked along the harbor, the first person she saw was young Jim Widdicombe, one of the "footpads" she had hired.

114

"Oh, my lady," he said, turning beet red. "I am sorry me and Peter did not come, like. 'Twas like this, ma'am. Father, he says to me, he says, that there's this here eddicated pig a-showing his tricks at the fair in Penryn. Well, that there pig fair drove everything out o' our heads, and me and Peter went over. 'Twas a wunnerful sage animal. You never did see the like. Could count up to ten, which is more 'n me nor Peter can."

"You will be glad to know," said Yvonne icily, "that while you and Peter were consorting with an educated pig, two *real* footpads set on me and Miss Cottingham."

"So's I heard," said Jim, staring at her in openmouthed admiration. "Two o' the worst villains in the county. 'Tis said you shot the one. I says to Peter, I says, happen we were right not to go. Might have been shot as well. It was God lookin' arter us, if you take my meaning."

"I will take my money back," said Yvonne with some asperity.

"Have it right here. My little brother, Ebenezer, we forgot to tell him not to go, us not remembering on account o' the pig, which is why he went to the castle. So you see, ma'am, if he hadn't gone, like, chances are you might have been seriously dead."

Yvonne sighed impatiently as she took the money from him. She extracted a shilling and told Jim to give it to his young brother. She was about to turn away when a thought struck her.

"Tell me, Jim," she said, "have you ever heard tell of anyone trying the same sort of trick in these parts? That is, anyone telling any of the local boys to dress up like pirates or brigands to give me a fright?"

"No, ma'am. Frightening a governess is one thing," said Jim, "but frightening the quality's a hanging matter. No one would dare."

"And so you are — how shall I put it — respectable and God-fearing?"

"Yes, 'cept for those in the Kennel."

"What is the Kennel?"

Jim lowered his voice and looked about nervously. "It's a collection o' huts along to the north o' Trewent. Nasty, dirty bunch lives there. Gets their living from pickin' things off the beach. Folks say hereabouts they might be wreckers."

"Wreckers?"

"Folk what shine a light from the shore to lure ships wi' cargo onto the rocks."

"You remember hearing how my governess and I were set upon by brigands?"

"Yes, my lady. Militia searched the whole of Trewent."

"But did they search this other place . . . this Kennel?"

"First place they went. Found nothing."

"I should like to see this place."

Jim began to back away. "Wot? The Kennel! I

dursn't go there. 'Tain't no place for a decent body."

"Oh, very well," said Yvonne. "But do not ever tell anyone I tried to hire you to pretend to be footpads."

"More 'n my life's worth," said Jim fervently. "His lordship might think we was in league with them ruffians."

"That he might," agreed Yvonne. "But hear this, Jim Widdicombe; it is just as well your young brother has more sense than you!"

Jim grinned sheepishly, bobbed his head, tugged his forelock, and slouched away.

Yvonne set out, back toward the castle.

But for the first time she felt afraid to be out on her own. The attack by the footpads had shocked her much more than her capture by the brigands. Every bush was a robber and every humped rock a crouched footpad waiting to spring.

A seagull called sharply from overhead, sending her heart jumping into her mouth.

She was nearing the castle when, once more, she saw the dark shape of a boat bobbing on the water in the cliffs below the castle. So it followed she could not have been mistaken that other time, whatever Patricia might say.

The winding cliff path dipped down into the hollow. She was just at the top of the dip when the black bulk of a man rose up in front of her.

Yvonne screamed and turned to run.

Strong arms caught her and held her. She

kicked back viciously and struggled and cursed in French until above the roaring in her ears she heard a familiar voice say sharply, "Yvonne! It is I. Anselm."

With a little broken sob, she turned about and leaned against him, feeling safe and secure and at home.

He gave her a little shake and held her away from him.

"You gave me the fright of my life," he said, "when I returned from Penryn and found you missing. Where were you?"

"I went for a walk to the village," mumbled Yvonne.

"After your experience today, you went out *alone?*"

Yvonne hung her head.

"Gustave said you had asked him to accompany you to the village," he went on when she did not reply. "He quite rightly refused, feeling you had had enough shocks and excursions for one day. He felt sure you had returned to the castle and not gone out again. But I think I know you better. I came in search of you. Why did you go to the village?"

"I felt shaken and uneasy. I wanted some fresh air," mumbled Yvonne.

He tilted her chin up and she could see the white gleam of his teeth as he grinned down at her.

"Liar," he mocked. "They were *real* footpads who attacked you and not some deep dark plot of Miss Cottingham, I should have thought the fright they gave you would have been enough to keep you indoors for weeks."

"I know they were real," said Yvonne sharply. "Who should know better than I?"

"Yes, you with your pistol. If, as you say, you were so strictly chaperoned, how did you come to be so expert in the use of firearms?"

"My grandfather taught me," said Yvonne. "In these troubled times, he said, it was important every young lady should know how to defend herself."

"A remarkable man. Well, come along, Yvonne. Since it is obvious you are not going to tell me why you went to the village, you leave me to assume you are romancing some poor lad."

"Not I!" exclaimed Yvonne, falling into step beside him. "What is this place — the Kennel?"

"A nasty hamlet full of nasty people."

"But when the brigands attacked me, no one at the castle could seem to think who might be to blame, and yet it appears you have a whole community of villains living nearby."

"Any villains who would attempt to abduct two ladies from Trewent Castle are of a breed unknown on this coast. Anyone from the Kennel would know it would be the first place we would search."

"Still . . ."

"No, Yvonne," he said. "No. You are not to go to the Kennel."

Yvonne gave a little shrug. He looked at her suspiciously, his eyes glinting down at her in the moonlight, but those black eyes of hers were unreadable.

"What of these fairies that local people believe in," said Yvonne, changing the subject. "People hereabouts are very superstitious, I think."

They were quite near the castle. The air was warm and sweet, and the night smells of crushed thyme and roses from the castle gardens appeared to heighten the viscount's senses, and he was sharply conscious of that dainty, voluptuous little body of Yvonne's so very close to his own.

"Me, I do not believe in fairies," said Yvonne.

Then she let out a terrified scream and threw herself into the viscount's arms as a cloud of winged creatures rose out of the heather and flew straight at her face.

"It's moths," he said, holding her tightly. "Only a type of moth we have about here."

Yvonne, who had burrowed her head against his chest, peeped nervously around his sheltering arms. "Not fairies?" she asked timidly.

"No, my sweet idiot," he said, smiling down at her. "Only moths."

She looked up at him, her eyes great dark pools and her mouth soft, young, and vulnerable. He felt a tremendous surge of passion mixed with an almost unbearable sweetness.

His arms dropped to his side and he said in a voice that did not sound like his own, "It is late. We are nearly home."

Yvonne muttered something that sounded like a French curse.

The air between them crackled with tension.

"I shall show you the diamonds if you would like," he said to try to dispel the strained atmosphere. "Would that please you?"

Yvonne gave a little laugh. "I am a woman, my lord. Of course I should like to see the Anselm diamonds."

They walked around to the front of the castle, and the viscount rang the bell for the gatekeeper. The tall iron spiked gates had been closed for the night.

As they walked side by side into the castle grounds, Yvonne looked up at the ugly bulk of Trewent Castle and felt for the first time she was coming home.

And for the first time a wistful little thought began to form in her mind. What if they were married? What if they were returning home together as man and wife?

Chapter Eight

The gloom of the castle hall closed around them, a now familiar smell of damp and woodsmoke and dried rose petals.

"This way," said the viscount rather curtly, almost as if he were already regretting the impulse that had prompted him to offer to show Yvonne the diamonds.

He led the way to a small door at the back of the hall. He searched on a ledge above the door until his groping hands found a key. He unlocked the door and stood aside to let Yvonne past.

Thin shafts of moonlight cut across the darkness of the room. The viscount gave an impatient exclamation, said, "Wait here," and retreated to the hall to find a lamp.

Soon the little room was bathed in a soft, golden glow. Yvonne looked about her curiously.

It was a pretty little room with comfortable chairs and an old-fashioned sofa upholstered in white and gold chintz. There was a portrait of a long-nosed lady in powdered hair and panniered gown above the fireplace. There were little occasional tables strewn with a haphazard array of embroidery patterns, silver boxes, fans, and china ornaments.

"This is the morning room," said the viscount. "I never use it."

"It is very pretty," said Yvonne, "and must get all the sun in the morning."

"You may use it if you like." He shrugged. "But keep the whereabouts of the diamonds to yourself."

"And where are they?" she teased. "I see no strongbox or jeweler's case."

He took the picture of the long-nosed lady down, revealing a square cupboard behind it. "Not a very good place," he said over his shoulder. "But since no one knows the whereabouts of the diamonds except me — and now you — I see no reason to journey to London to buy one of Mr. Chubb's safes."

He opened the cupboard and lifted down a large, heavy leather-covered box.

Yvonne looked in awe as he lifted the lid. Diamonds flashed and blazed.

"How beautiful," she whispered.

"They are very heavy," he said, "and cold. There is a tiara, rings, a necklace, earrings, and brooches. Come here, and let us see how you look in all this finery."

He lifted the heavy tiara and placed it on her head, then the necklace about her neck, and stood back to survey the effect.

The result was breathtaking. She looked like

some princess out of a fairy tale.

"You may wear them at the ball," he heard himself saying.

"Yes," said Yvonne almost absentmindedly, because she was dreamily watching the expression of admiration in his blue eyes.

Then something made her look over his shoulder and she turned pale.

"A face! A face at the window!" she cried.

He went over and fumbled with the rusty catch of the latticed window and threw it open. Like the library, the morning room looked out onto the terrace.

The terrace gleamed white and empty in the moonlight.

"Idiot," said the viscount. "Go to bed, my child. You are weary and still shocked. But first come here and let me put these baubles away."

Yvonne was still shaken. "I saw a face," she kept saying over and over again, and he took off the jewels and returned them to their box. "I *did*."

"These little leaded panes of glass play strange tricks with the eyes," he said. "Go to sleep. Bright sunlight and a new day will banish all your frights and fantasies."

Yvonne lay awake that night for a long time. *Was* she imagining trickery, deception, faces, and frauds on all sides? She had tried the door of Patricia's room, but it had been locked. All she knew was that she was becoming afraid. Very afraid and apprehensive.

But the bright sunlight and bustle and excitement just before the ball somewhat restored Yvonne's spirits. Patricia was calm, almost placid, but still obviously much shaken from their adventure. She could not have felt well enough the previous night to go running around outside the castle, looking in at the windows. It was the day before the ball, and Yvonne's restlessness soon returned and her desire to see this place called the Kennel grew.

She decided she would be safe enough if she rode there, and armed herself with her pistol. The difficulty would be in getting her horse out of the stables without alerting Gustave or any of the stable staff.

At last, she hit on a plan and asked Gustave to accompany her. Instead of riding to the north in the direction of the Kennel, she set off east, across the moors. When they had cantered about a mile from the castle, she affected to have a sneezing fit.

"I must return and find my vinaigrette and a handkerchief, Gustave," Yvonne called.

Her groom obediently wheeled his placid mare in the direction of the castle.

"No, Gustave," called Yvonne. "Wait here. You cannot ride fast enough."

Before Gustave could protest, she was off like the wind, and he knew his own bad horsemanship, combined with his slow mount, would prevent him from catching up with her.

Suddenly suspicious, he urged his slow horse up on top of one of the little hills on the moorland, and, screwing up his eyes against the sun, he watched the little flying figure that was Yvonne.

She rode almost to the castle walls and then veered away to the north, in the direction of the village of Trewent.

Gustave set out for the castle as fast as he could manage to go. He knew where his duty lay.

Yvonne rode at full gallop until she was above the village, which nestled in a cove at the foot of the cliffs. She did not go down into the village but carried on to the north, where she was sure she would recognize the place called the Kennel when she saw it.

She slowed her mount to a walking pace. A thin veil of cloud now hid the sun. The air was warm and heavy, and everything was a strange pearl gray. The sea was a sheet of motionless gray glass, and there was hardly a breath of wind.

She plodded on and was beginning to wonder whether she had passed the Kennel, whether it might lie down at the foot of the cliffs at the bottom of some concealed path, when she heard the thud of hooves in the distance.

She looked to right and left, but there was nowhere she could conceal herself or her horse. Fear sharpened her wits. The approaching rider was coming at such speed that to flee would be useless. Her mount was already tired from the gallop.

She swung her horse around, prepared to face whoever was coming, and drew her loaded pistol out of her saddlebag and laid it across the pommel of her saddle.

Then she gave a sigh, half of relief, half of exasperation, as the approaching horseman turned out to be her guardian.

She dropped her pistol back into the saddlebag as he reined in beside her, his eyes hard and angry.

"A stupid trick, Yvonne de la Falaise," he said. "Have you lost your wits? You will return with me immediately. Gustave told me you had tricked him, and I *knew* you meant to disobey me and come here."

"Where is this Kennel?" asked Yvonne, seemingly indifferent to his fury.

"Half a mile ahead."

"Please, now that you are here, cannot I just *look?*" begged Yvonne.

He surveyed the slim figure in the elegant riding dress and his anger left him. He had been so afraid she might have landed in some scrape that visions of giving her a good hiding had consumed his thoughts as he pursued her. But now that she was safe and well, he found he could not continue to rage against her.

"Very well, you selfish child," he said. "But I doubt if we shall see any of the inhabitants.

They disappear as soon as any stranger approaches."

They rode on side by side until the viscount pointed his riding crop at a partially concealed track leading down the cliffs. He swung his horse down it, and Yvonne followed behind, seeing a huddle of huts far down below on a shingle beach.

What an odd day it was, thought Yvonne. All color seemed to have been drained out of the landscape. The huts were dark gray against the pearl gray of the unnaturally still sea.

There were figures grouped about a boat on the shore, and other figures, foreshortened by the height of Yvonne's precipitous view, clustered around the huts.

Then one of the figures turned and pointed toward them. One minute they were all there, and the next they had gone, having melted away into the gray landscape.

By the time the viscount and Yvonne rode along the beach to the Kennel, there was no one in sight except an old man, a huddled bundle of rags sitting on a rock, staring out to sea.

"Well, this is the Kennel," said the viscount, "and now that you have seen it, I suggest we return to the castle."

But Yvonne was already approaching the old man on the beach. "Good afternoon, sir," she said, forcing herself to speak in a normal tone of voice, for it was tempting to whisper in the middle of all this unearthly quiet.

His rheumy old eyes swiveled up to meet hers and then turned back to resume gazing out to sea.

"Where is everyone?" went on Yvonne brightly.

"Hereabouts," said the old man laconically. "Don't like strangers. Better run along, missie, 'fore Black Jack gets you."

"Black Jack," said the viscount in a bored voice, "was hanged for his crimes ages ago."

"But his ghost walks, guv'nor."

"Black Jack?" Yvonne frowned and then her face cleared. "Oh, the pirate."

"Yes'm."

"I don't believe in ghosts," said Yvonne.

"Come along, Yvonne," said the viscount, walking back toward where their horses were tethered.

"Course they walk," said the old man. "Ain't I seen Black Jack's granddaughter?"

"Tell me about her," said Yvonne, who loved stories.

"Can't," said the old man peevishly. "Ain't got no 'baccy. Can't think without 'baccy."

Yvonne drew a shilling from the pocket of her riding dress and held it out. "This will buy you tobacco."

He took the shilling in one grimy, arthritic paw, examined it carefully, and stowed it away somewhere among his filthy rags.

"Well, she was the prettiest thing you ever

did see," said the old man. "We ain't used to prettiness in the Kennel. Women here is most squat and dark. Black Jack was dead, and his son married Kate Harty, a slut. They had this daughter."

"Called?" prompted Yvonne eagerly.

"Called Ellen — Ellen Tremayne — that bein' Jack's family name. Well, one night there was this gurt storm, and Kate war out on the rocks with her light, looking for wreckage." He peered up at Yvonne slyly, and Yvonne had a sudden vivid picture of a ruthless woman waving a lantern to lure the ships onto the rocks.

"A big merchantman foundered, just out there. None o' the crew survived."

Yvonne shuddered. She had a feeling that none of the crew had been allowed to survive.

"One dyin' sailor, he says there's a chest o' gold in the captain's cabin. Kate went diving for it. 'Tis said she never found it, though her body was washed up . . . drownded," added the old man with horrible relish.

"Yvonne!" called the viscount.

"Go on," urged Yvonne, ignoring him.

"Next day, arter we buried her, Black Jack's son and baby Ellen disappeared. Folks about here said they'd got the gold, see. But they must have been killed. 'Cos I seed her ghost, missie."

A strong grip took hold of Yvonne's arm and swung her about. "When I tell you to come, you will obey me," said the viscount.

Yvonne jerked her arm free, rubbing it and glaring up at him in a fury.

"You have no right to treat me so roughly."

"I have every right. I am your guardian."

"I, my lord, am going to find a good lusty husband who will give you the thrashing you deserve. You are a monstrous bully. Oh, look!"

While they had been arguing, the old man had shuffled off. Moving with an odd crabwise gait, he disappeared between the huts. "Now I shall never hear the end of the story," mourned Yvonne. "It was fascinating. Ghosts and pirates and —"

"How much did you give him?"

"A shilling."

"My dear child, give him a sovereign and he will invent tales for a month."

They rode back to the castle, each thoroughly disappointed with the other.

The viscount was thinking Yvonne was nothing more than a willful child who disobeyed him because she preferred to listen to the maunderings of a dirty, senile old man. Yvonne thought the viscount stupidly pigheaded and overbearing and heartily pitied any woman who might be fool enough to marry him.

They parted in the castle hall without speaking, Yvonne to her sitting room and the viscount to the library.

But he found he could not remain angry with

her for long. He wanted to see her smile at him again, to see her look up into his face with that glow in her large eyes.

He decided to take the diamonds up to her so that she might have them ready for the ball on the morrow.

He unlocked the door of the morning room and lifted the portrait down from over the fireplace. He opened the cupboard and took out the box. It felt strangely light. He threw back the lid.

Empty.

His heart felt heavy. He sat down on the nearest chair.

Surely no one else in the castle knew of the whereabouts of the diamonds except him — and Yvonne.

A sudden burst of rage spurred him to action.

He sent for Fairbairn and demanded that everyone in the castle be summoned to the hall. Miss Cottingham, too, must be helped downstairs. Everyone had to be present.

When they were all gathered, he stood up on the staircase, looking down at them. Yvonne was there, wide-eyed and curious; Miss Cottingham, pale and tired.

"Listen, all of you," he said. "The Anselm diamonds have been taken from their hiding place. You are all to go outside while the castle is searched."

He looked down at their faces. He must have

people he could trust to help him with the search. Most of the castle servants had been in service with the late viscount. Only two of the footmen, some of the outdoor staff, and three of the housemaids had been hired that year. Then there were all the workers who had been drafted in to help with the arrangements for the ball — caterers, musicians, builders, and decorators.

"Mrs. Pardoe and Fairbairn, step forward," he commanded.

The butler and the housekeeper edged to the front of the crowd.

"You will both help me in my search," he said. "Everyone else is to gather outside on the castle lawn and stay there until I tell you to do otherwise. Make sure there is no one in the stables, or in any of the outside living quarters either."

Yvonne followed the others out. She remembered that strange doorway in the cellar. Should she tell the viscount about it? But he would want to know what she had been doing down there, and he might suspect it was she who had rung the alarm bell.

They all waited outside for what seemed like an age.

Inside, Fairbairn and Mrs. Pardoe reported to the viscount that they had searched all of the servants' rooms.

"We still have the other rooms to search," said the viscount harshly. "Come with me. We will start with my ward's bedroom."

Fairbairn and Mrs. Pardoe exchanged startled glances, but they followed him to Yvonne's bedroom.

They watched nervously as the viscount rummaged through closets, tossing gowns and mantles over his shoulder in his haste. Drawers of lingerie were upended on the floor.

The grim, set look did not leave his face.

"Don't seem to be anything here, my lord," ventured Mrs. Pardoe timidly.

"I have not finished." He stood with his hands on his hips, surveying the wreck of the pretty bedchamber.

Then with one quick move, he ripped the bedclothes from the bed and raised the feather mattress.

Fire and ice gleamed and sparkled and shone. The Anselm diamonds blazed up at him in all their wicked glory.

Mrs. Pardoe stifled an exclamation and put her hands to her mouth.

The viscount stooped to scoop up the gems. He bundled them into a large huckaback towel and gave them to Fairbairn. "Take these . . . baubles . . . to the morning room," he said heavily. "You know where the key is. Leave them on a table, lock the door behind you, and bring the key to me. You will say I made a mistake. You will say I had the jewels all along. Do you understand?"

They both nodded dumbly.

"Mrs. Pardoe, tell everyone to go about their duties and then help Miss Cottingham to her bedchamber. Then when the fuss has died down, go quietly to my ward and tell her to attend me in the library."

For the next half hour the castle was in a buzz of excitement, the servants making the most of this brief respite from their duties. Then the men who had been erecting the large marquees on the lawn went back to their work, the orchestra who had been rehearsing in the upstairs saloon tuned up again, and the caterers who had traveled down from Exeter went back to their consultations with the chef.

Soon the urgency of all of the preparations for the ball took over.

Mrs. Pardoe found Yvonne standing in the middle of her bedchamber, looking in dismay at the mess.

"I shall send two of the girls to put everything away, my lady," said Mrs. Pardoe.

"But why *my* room?" asked Yvonne, amazed.

"Everyone's room was searched," said the housekeeper, not meeting her eyes. "His lordship sends his compliments and would like to see you in the library, my lady, as soon as possible."

A delicate pink suffused Yvonne's cheeks, and her large eyes sparkled. "Looked as if she was going to her wedding," Mrs. Pardoe gloomily reported later to the butler.

Yvonne sat down at her dressing table and

arranged her curls to her satisfaction. She sprayed on a new perfume called Miss in Her Teens, and then, satisfied she was looking her best, she ran down to the library.

All her anger at the viscount for having lectured her that afternoon, for having searched her room, fled.

She had just one glorious thought in her head. She was to see him. Her beloved guardian.

He was standing at the library window, staring out to sea, when she entered.

He turned slowly around as he heard her light step.

Yvonne flinched before the blaze of rage in his blue eyes. His mouth was a hard line.

"Well?" he demanded. "And what have you to say for yourself?"

"Oh, I thought all that was over," said Yvonne, disappointed. "Now it appears you are still furious with me because I wanted to go to the Kennel."

"I should have left you there with your own kind, you thieving little jade."

"Thieving . . . ?"

"Yes, thieving," raged the viscount. "The Anselm diamonds, as you very well know, were found where you had hidden them . . . under your mattress."

"I did not take them," shouted Yvonne. "They must have been left there to incriminate me! Patricia . . ."

He took two steps forward and seized her by

the shoulders and shook her until her teeth rattled.

"Patricia," he said, sneering. "Your governess can barely walk, and it is doubtful if she will even be well enough to attend the ball tomorrow. *You* are not the scapegoat. Miss Cottingham is the scapegoat for your vulgar, detestable behavior. This is what comes of taking someone *French* into my home. Of all the treacherous races in the world —"

"No!" screamed Yvonne. "No. I am innocent."

"Don't be a fool," he said with a flat weariness that was more terrifying to Yvonne than his rage. "You will attend the ball as we planned, Yvonne. You will behave prettily and dance and smile. You will not wear the diamonds. After the ball, and after I am sure there has been no scandal, we shall remove to London and a marriage shall be arranged for you."

"You would sell me off?"

"Gladly. It will cost me dear, but it will be worth every penny. Get out of here, and stay out of my sight until tomorrow."

He sat down and buried his face in his hands.

"Anselm," pleaded Yvonne. "Pay me heed. . . ."

He raised a tortured face and looked at her steadily. "Get out," he said in a low voice. "The sight of you makes me sick."

Yvonne could bear no more. She fled to her bedchamber, only to find the maids busily putting everything away. She turned and ran, ran out of the castle and straight to Gustave's room. He was not there, so she threw herself down on his narrow bed and cried her eyes out.

When dusk fell, as Gustave slowly opened the door and stood looking down at the hunched figure on the bed, she was still crying.

He knelt down beside her, demanding roughly to know what had happened. Still Yvonne continued to sob.

He poured some brandy into a thick tumbler and held it to her lips, thrusting it against her mouth, coaxing and threatening by turns until she drank some of the spirit.

Bit by bit the story came out, disjointed, broken by sobs. Gustave listened, appalled.

"We should never have come to this accursed country," he said. "They hate us because we are French."

"But, Gustave, I have not met with any un-kindness at Trewent, nor have you. England is at war with France. It is natural they should *say* bad things about the French."

Gustave sniffed and poured himself some brandy.

"And who would play such an evil trick on me?" demanded Yvonne.

"I told you," said Gustave. "Any of them. They hate the French."

"But listen, Gustave, when Lord Anselm was first showing me the jewels, I thought I saw a face at the window. But when he looked out, there was no one there. Gustave, it *must* be Patricia. I feel it is all to do with her."

Gustave gave a very Gallic shrug. "Me, I think it is the French haters. Do you know what they call you behind your back, milady? Frenchie."

"That is . . . is not so bad," said Yvonne cautiously.

"You need a good night's sleep, milady. His lordship will see sense in the morning. I shall speak to him."

"No, you must not bring yourself to his attention. He might accuse you of being in league with me, and then he will send you away. I could not bear that, Gustave. You are all I have. Oh, Gustave, his lordship says that after the ball he is going to take me to London and arrange a marriage for me."

Gustave's face brightened. "That is well. That is the French way. You will have your own household, milady, and your old Gustave along with you."

"I don't want an arranged marriage," said Yvonne, beginning to cry again.

"You want Lord Anselm," said Gustave harshly. "Even after this, you want his lordship. You cannot have him. Besides, a man who does not trust you is not worth your love."

After she had left, Gustave shaved and put on his best livery and presented himself at the castle, demanding to see Lord Anselm.

Fairbairn shook his head gloomily, saying he

doubted that Lord Anselm would see anyone, but returned some moments later, looking surprised, and ushered Gustave into the library.

Lord Anselm was sitting behind his desk. Gustave stood in front of him, noticing the new harsh lines cutting down either side of the viscount's mouth.

"Well?" demanded the viscount.

"Milady did not take your jewels," said Gustave, standing rigidly to attention.

"Oh, no? Then who did?" asked the viscount sweetly.

"That I do not know, milord. I have known milady since she was a baby, and I, Gustave Bouvet, tell you this. She could not . . . She is . . ." His English ran out, and he looked at the viscount, fumbling for the right words.

"Your loyalty does you credit, Gustave," said the viscount in perfect French. "But the evidence is damning."

"Evidence does not matter," said Gustave, speaking in his native tongue. "Trust is what matters. Trust and loyalty and the use of one's common sense."

The viscount sighed. "I saw you, Gustave, for I hoped against hope you would give me some material proof of her innocence. Loyalty blinds you. I know my ward. I know *women!* Pah. I do not think she planned any villainy or to keep the jewels forever. They sparkled; she wanted them like a child wants a glittering toy. She could not even wait until the ball."

"You do not understand. She is French, not English, and therefore much older than her years. Milady is not stupid. Let us suppose she wanted the jewels for some reason. Then she would not hide them under her mattress. She would *know* there would be a search of the rooms. She would hide them outside the castle, somewhere you would not think of looking."

The viscount frowned. "In Portugal," he said, "I gather your late master ran out of funds. You must have needed every penny, and yet Yvonne de la Falaise obviously spent a great deal of money on clothes. That shows a frivolous and heedless spirit."

"The clothes were made by a dressmaker in Lisbon to milady's designs," said Gustave. "This dressmaker, she had a gift, a talent, but she was not a great couturier and did not charge high prices. It was milady who discovered her talent. Oh, milord, you should have seen her this evening in my little room, crying fit to break your heart, had you but heard her."

"Enough. You may go. Do not trouble me again until you have something to tell me other than your own opinion of her character."

Gustave searched the viscount's face for some signs of softening, but his eyes were hard and implacable.

Yvonne's broken sobs sounded in his ears. He decided to try harder. "Milady suspects her governess of trying to discredit her," said Gustave.

141

The viscount gave an impatient exclamation.

"Me, too — I think she has become obsessed with this Miss Cottingham. But think! Miss Cottingham lied about her references. Understandable, you might think, since she explained she had no other alternative. She needed the work, and that work she could not get without references. So all is forgiven, and yet nothing is done to try to find out if she is really what she says she is."

"Why on earth would Miss Cottingham try to discredit Yvonne?"

Gustave looked at the viscount out of the corners of his eyes. "Perhaps because — I repeat only the rumors, you see — perhaps it is because this governess has hopes of marrying you herself and fears milady might take away your affections."

"You go too far," said the viscount, turning red.

"Then I will go further," said Gustave stoutly, "and you must forgive an old and loyal servant for speaking so plain. I am an old man and have seen much. If you do not go very carefully, you may find one day you have lost a treasure of value — of more value than the Anselm diamonds or of the crown jewels."

The viscount pointed to the door.

"Go!" he said.

And with bowed shoulders and lagging footsteps, Gustave went.

As he crossed the shadowy hall to the main

door, he heard a light step up on the first landing and swung around. There came the quick, light patter of footsteps and the glimpse of a long skirt whisking away out of sight.

Milady, thought Gustave. Eavesdropping. He wondered whether he should go after her but decided against it. The viscount had said nothing he could repeat that might cheer her.

And, unaware that Yvonne had fallen into an exhausted sleep half an hour before, he opened the door of the castle and let himself out into the night.

Chapter Nine

Yvonne de la Falaise stood beside her guardian at the entrance to the marquee on the lawn where the guests were to assemble. There were three marquees, the one where the company was to be received, another where wine and food were to be served, and the third for dancing.

Many of the guests who were to stay overnight had already arrived.

Yvonne had kept to her sitting room for most of the day. Patricia had knocked at her door several times, demanding to know if all was well, but Yvonne could not bear to see her. Somehow she felt Patricia had been responsible for her disgrace. Why she should continue to suspect the governess, Yvonne did not know, but suspect her she did.

She had joined the viscount in the hall, and together they had walked to the entrance to the marquee where they were to receive their guests.

All her hurt and misery had returned full force at the sight of him, but she allowed none of it to show on her face. The viscount barely looked at her.

They stood side by side, smiling and shaking hands, each of them feeling thoroughly miserable.

Yvonne was wearing her finest gown. It consisted of a scarlet and gold tissue robe, trimmed with scarlet and gold, and worn over a petticoat of white satin, which was edged with scarlet and gold fringe. The front of the robe was fastened over the petticoat with gilt clasps so cleverly made that they looked like real gold. Yvonne had been grateful she had saved this favorite gown for the ball, but since the disgrace brought down on her by the taking of the diamonds, she gloomily felt it did not matter what she wore. She had dressed her hair in a severe coronet on top of her small head with gold ribbons threaded through the braids as her only ornament.

Beside her, Lord Anselm was wearing the latest thing in evening dress — black pantaloons that hugged his long legs like a second skin, stopping at midcalf to reveal a length of green and gold stocking. His coat was black, and his waistcoat was of white piqué with diamond studs. Diamonds blazed on his fingers and among the snowy folds of his cravat. As a concession to the old-fashioned ways of the country, he wore his thick fair hair powdered and confined at the nape of his neck with a black silk ribbon.

Despite her misery, Yvonne was amazed at the democracy of an English country ball. They were all there, from the lord-lieutenant of the county to the village milkmaid.

If only he would believe me, then I might enjoy all this, thought Yvonne later as she footed her way nimbly through the steps of a country dance with the baker's boy.

When Lord Anselm led Patricia Cottingham onto the floor for a waltz, Yvonne closed her eyes, stabbed with sudden jealousy and fierce longing.

He should have been holding her, Yvonne, and guiding *her* through the steps of this new exotic dance where the man clasped the woman about the waist.

Patricia was wearing her favorite blue silk, cut much too low at the bosom for a governess, thought Yvonne, smiling automatically at her own partner and wishing she were dead.

There went Patricia, floating in the viscount's arms, while she herself was clasped in the clumsy, sweaty embrace of the captain of the local militia.

Oh, horrors! The good captain was stammering out his wish to take her into supper.

Yvonne gave a sad little smile and accepted his invitation with as much grace as she could muster. If the point of this ball is to find me a husband, she thought as she shook out her napkin, then my guardian must be all about in his upper chambers. There is not one marriageable man here. They are either old and elegant or young and uncouth.

Then she became aware that the captain was talking about her adventures.

"It is thanks to you, my lady," he was saying, "that we caught those two footpads."

"Not at all," said Yvonne modestly. "Lord Anselm's arrival on the scene at the right moment did that."

"These are bad times," said the captain, fingering his military sideburns. "And that was not the first time you were attacked."

Now he had Yvonne's full attention.

"Tell me, Captain . . . ?"

"Jenkins, my lady."

"Tell me, Captain Jenkins. Is it not odd that brigands should attack two ladies on a sunny day?"

"Very odd," agreed the captain. "I have been puzzling over it. I thought it might be some of those ruffians who live in the Kennel. But they have been toothless for decades. No major piracy or crime since Black Jack was caught, and that was in my grandfather's time."

"What was also very strange," said Yvonne, "was that the boat, the *Trewent Castle*, was returned the next day."

"That makes it odder still. I could hardly believe it when I learned of its return. At first I thought Lord Anselm might have been holding a house party."

"What would that have to do with it?"

"I thought perhaps some young people might have dressed up as pirates to play a malicious joke on you. Feeling against the French runs high. It had the appearance of a charade."

"Is there much smuggling on this coast?"

"I believe there is some. I don't know who runs it, for no one has ever been caught. And there's no one around here with the brains to outwit the excisemen."

Yvonne, totally absorbed in questioning the captain, had, for the moment, forgotten about the disgrace of the Anselm diamonds. Her face was animated, and her beauty, which had been somewhat dimmed by misery, blazed out in the room.

No, she did not need diamonds to enhance her looks, thought the viscount. He studied her covertly while trying to pay attention to what Miss Cottingham was saying. He had a dim feeling that the governess deserved a setdown. Her gown was much too low, and her manner verged on boldness. Certainly everyone was drinking rather a lot, and all classes were mixing freely, so it would not occasion much comment, but it made the viscount feel decidedly uneasy.

"Sir Reginald is trying to catch your attention, Miss Cottingham," he said abruptly, and Patricia reluctantly turned to the gentleman on her other side. Sir Reginald looked gratified at her interest and somewhat surprised, for he had been comfortably enjoying his wine and had not been trying to speak to her at all.

Once the governess was engaged in conversation with Sir Reginald, the viscount heaved a sigh of relief and fell to studying Yvonne's face.

She was so very beautiful — and so very innocent. That new thought struck him forcibly as he watched her. She looked across the room as if aware of his glance, and their eyes locked and held.

Yvonne's expressive little face mirrored hurt, sadness, and bewilderment before she dropped her eyes, those ridiculously long eyelashes of hers fanning out over her cheeks.

No, thought the viscount, she did not take those jewels. Gustave is right. She is no fool. Had she taken them, she would have hidden them out on the moors or somewhere on the cliffs, but she would never have concealed them in her bedchamber.

He felt as if he had been looking at her the wrong way, looking at her through a distorting glass.

There were so many thoughts crowding into his mind all at once that he shook his head slightly as if to clear it.

When she had cried out there was a face at the window when they were both looking at the diamonds, he could swear her surprise and shock had been genuine. Then there was that mysterious kidnapping.

He looked at her face again. It was sad now, and drained of animation. There were faint violet bruises of fatigue under her eyes.

Why had he been so *determined* to believe her guilty? Why did he always *want* to believe the worst of her? Was it because the increasing attraction she held for him put his independence at risk?

He became aware that Miss Cottingham was trying to catch his attention, and he looked at her impatiently. Where now was the cool and calm governess he had once admired?

Her eyes were glowing with a soft light as she looked at him, and he felt she was deliberately leaning forward to expose even more of her bosom.

He had not noticed before, he reflected, how very white and sharp her teeth were.

She bit into a peach and cast a languishing — yes, *voluptuous* — look at him.

"Excuse me," he said abruptly.

Patricia watched while he rose from the table. Her eyes followed his tall figure as he strode down the room. They watched as he bent over his ward and said something. Then Yvonne rose and followed him out.

"Where are you taking me?" asked Yvonne when they were outside.

"I would like you to wear the Anselm diamonds," he said.

Yvonne stumbled, and he caught her arm to steady her.

"I might run away with them," she said bitterly.

"No, you would not, Yvonne, and I am a great fool to ever think you would steal them. Will you forgive me?"

"Yes," gasped Yvonne, lifting up her skirts and hurrying to keep up with his long strides. "What made you change your mind?"

He did not answer her until they were in the morning room.

As he lifted down the picture, he said, "It was your innocent face, my sweeting. I am also a fool to have left the diamonds in the same hiding place. Someone wished you ill. No, don't try to tell me it was Miss Cottingham. Although I now believe you innocent, it does not follow that I can believe her guilty. There is much anti-French feeling about."

"Frenchie — that is what they call me behind my back."

"That does not mean they don't like you," he said gently.

He opened the box and lifted out the tiara. "Stand still," he said.

"I do not think I want to wear them now," said Yvonne with a shiver.

"You will do as you are told. There!" He set the tiara carefully on her head.

"How heavy it feels," whispered Yvonne.

"Now turn around."

She felt the heavy, cold weight of the diamonds as he slipped a necklace about her neck.

"Now, look at me," he commanded.

She turned and obediently looked up at him.

151

The diamonds blazed with a fierce fire, with a life of their own.

He felt a surge of possession. This beauty was his ward, wearing his family jewels.

"You look . . . exotic," he said. "Come, Yvonne, let me show you in all your glory to my guests."

She put her hand on his arm, and he led her from the room, carelessly leaving the rest of the jewels in their open box on the table.

As they passed through the hall, they could hear the faint strains of music filtering in from outside. Yvonne stopped and looked about her.

"What is it?" he asked, stopping as well.

"Menace," said Yvonne slowly. "I feel it. Someone hates me."

He looked down at her curiously and then his eyes probed into the shadows on the hall.

"There is no one here," he said. "You are overnice in your sensibilities. This was once a prison. The most evil malefactors were put down in the dungeons below the cellars — the lesser in what are now the cellars, and the debtors and French prisoners up here."

"Do you mean these were all cells?" asked Yvonne, looking about her. "And what French prisoners?"

"Spies. There were always spies along this coast. The old viscount had all the cells knocked together and made into bedrooms, drawing rooms, saloons, and so on. Perhaps that is why I like the library. It was the old prison governor's room. No one was ever locked up in there."

"There is something I must tell you," said Yvonne urgently. "You will not be angry with me?"

His face softened as he looked at her. "I do not think I could find it in me to be angry at anything you might say."

"Perhaps," said Yvonne cautiously. "But it was a very wicked thing to do. I thought you were going to propose marriage to Patricia, and I did not think that would be a very good thing. So I rang the fire bell."

"So that was you, you minx! I should have known."

"But listen! When I was in the cellars, I heard someone approaching, and it turned out to be Fairbairn. I hid behind a barrel in the corner of the cellar. As I pressed back against the wall for fear he might see me, I felt it give way. It proved to be a concealed door that led to the old dungeons below."

"Are you sure? They were sealed off in my grandfather's time, for the level of the sea had risen and had started to flood the old lower dungeons at high tide."

"I did not have a light with me," said Yvonne. "I groped my way through the opening. There were stairs leading down. I thought it might have been an old escape route. When I first heard the diamonds had gone missing, I meant to tell you, because I thought someone might have entered the castle from outside by that way."

"We shall examine it together in the morning," he said. "I cannot understand how Fairbairn missed it."

"There was a piece of canvas pasted over it, painted to match the wall on either side."

"Strange. Let us return to our guests and forget about it for now. These old places are riddled with unexpected tunnels and passages. There were a few escapes from here in the old days that were never explained. It stands to reason there might be some secret passages that do not appear in the original plans of the castle."

"And you forgive me?"

"I told you, my chit, that I do not believe you took the diamonds."

"Not that. I mean for ringing the fire bell."

The viscount reflected with wonder that he *had* been about to propose marriage to Patricia on that day. It was like looking back on the actions of a stranger.

"I forgive you."

"Were you going to ask Patricia to marry you?"

"No," lied the viscount. "Yvonne . . ."

He put his hands on her shoulders and looked down at her.

"Do you consider me *very* old?"

"No, m-my lord," said Yvonne with a catch in her voice.

"We must spend more time together, my chuck. Do you understand? We must be sure. The man you want now may not be the man you will want when you are older."

"*Baise-moi,*" said Yvonne in a low voice.

"I cannot continue these familiarities with my own ward."

"Idiot! Then your ward will kiss *you.*"

She rose on tiptoe and he felt her lips, warm and soft, pressing against his own. Passion rocked him on his heels, a passion so violent, so shocking, that he wrenched his mouth free. Yvonne looked up at him, her eyes wide and dark with disappointment.

"As I said," he remarked in as casual a voice as he could manage, "it is important we should get to know each other better."

But he felt deeply shaken as he led her out of the castle. She was young and innocent and virginal. He felt like a depraved old lecher. How could so young a girl who must surely dream of pure and spiritual romance understand the blazing red-hot passion of a man who only wanted to rip every shred of clothing from her body and make love to her for hour after hour?

Yvonne's jewels caused a sensation. People crowded around to exclaim and admire, although many young ladies of the county looked daggers at Yvonne. It was well known the Anselm jewels were traditionally worn by the Anselm bride. This Frenchie had stolen a march on them all.

"Have you any dances left?" the viscount asked Yvonne.

"Only a waltz," said Yvonne.

"But there is a Mr. Grummings's name written in that space."

Yvonne turned red with embarrassment. She had invented the fictitious Mr. Grummings in the hope that the viscount would dance with her after all.

"He has the gout," she said, "and cannot dance."

The viscount gave her an amused look as he wrote his name over that of Mr. Grummings. "You must introduce me to him. I do not remember inviting him."

"Oh, here is Patricia," said Yvonne. "You must have promised her another dance. How is your head, *dear* Patricia? You made a remarkable recovery."

"I am still feeling rather dizzy," said Patricia, and, indeed, she did look very pale.

"Then let me take you for some refreshment instead of dancing," said the viscount, and then cursed, since it would mean half an hour of intimate conversation in Patricia's company.

As they walked into the refreshment tent, he could only be glad that she appeared more subdued than she had earlier.

"It was a noble and courageous gesture to let Yvonne wear the Anselm diamonds," said Patricia. She drank a full glass of wine in one gulp.

"There was nothing noble and courageous

about my behavior," he said. "I should never have suspected my ward in the first place."

"But how could you not? The diamonds were found under her mattress."

"How did you know that?" he asked sharply. "Only Fairbairn and Mrs. Pardoe knew where they were found. As far as everyone else is concerned, I made a mistake.

"So, I repeat, who could possibly have told you? And why should you find it a noble and courageous gesture when my ward had not been accused of theft?"

"Yvonne must have told me," said Patricia, looking at him in surprise.

"I shall ask her."

"My lord, Yvonne is scatterbrained and does not remember from one moment to the next what she has said. Like a magpie."

"You imply that she takes bright objects — just like a magpie?"

"No, no," said Patricia wretchedly. "That is not what I meant. Oh, my poor head."

He sat looking at his untouched glass of wine, his mind racing. Mrs. Pardoe would not have told the governess of the theft, nor would Fairbairn. He was sure Yvonne would not have told the governess either — unless, perhaps, to accuse her of having taken the jewels herself.

"At one time, my lord," said Patricia, drinking another glass of wine as if it were lemonade, "you were kind enough to say I could always make my home at Trewent Castle, even after Yvonne married. You started to say I could stay as your . . . but, if you remember, we were interrupted. What were you about to say?"

The viscount felt trapped. He felt as if some woman had surfaced from his far past with a claim on his affections. And yet he had wanted to marry her. He had wanted to marry her because she had seemed so calm, so unruffled, so passionless.

I cannot remember telling a lie in my life, he thought, and yet this evening I have already lied to Yvonne and I am about to lie again to her governess.

Aloud he said, "I meant to add, as my pensioner. On reflection, however, I see you are quite right. You could not possibly stay with me were I still unwed. But I own some cottages on the outskirts of Penryn, and one even now stands vacant."

"My lord," said Patricia in a thin, hard voice, "I do not believe you."

"I admit it is unusual and generous to pension a servant who is neither old nor infirm," he said, deliberately misunderstanding her, "but I owe you much."

Patricia had turned very white indeed. He took her wineglass from her hand and put it on the table away from her. "You must not drink so much," he said. "I am afraid the blow to your head was more severe than we had at first thought. You should not have attended the ball."

"No, my lord," said Patricia in a flat voice. "But I had hopes . . . hopes, my lord, that . . ."

He rose hurriedly to his feet. "You must forgive me, Miss Cottingham, I have neglected my ward for too long."

Patricia sat very still, watching him go. Then she reached for the decanter and poured herself another glass of wine.

Yvonne was beginning to think the viscount had forgotten their dance, but as soon as the waltz was announced, he appeared at her side.

"Can you waltz?" he asked. "Perhaps it was considered too *fast* a dance in staid Portugal."

"Oh, I learned the steps," said Yvonne airily. "In secret."

He placed his hand at her waist, marveling at the feeling of longing and desire that simple touch brought. Yvonne had been feeling tired and depressed. The diamonds weighed heavily on her small head, and the weight of the necklace dragged at her neck.

But at his touch she forgot all her fatigue and discomfort and floated off in his arms.

This must be love, thought Yvonne. This wanting to dance forever, this feeling of having come home.

They did not speak, although each longed to say words of love. Yvonne was kept silent by a fear the viscount might take her in dislike or be alarmed if he began to guess how deeply she had fallen in love with him. The viscount was still worried that young Yvonne viewed him only as some sort of uncle figure — fun to tease, fun to flirt with, but nothing more.

All too quickly the waltz spun to an end and Yvonne's next partner was waiting to claim her.

All her fatigue returned. Would the ball *never* end? Yvonne danced on and on, comforted a little by noticing the viscount no longer chose to dance but circulated among the older guests who were content to sit and watch.

There was no sign of Patricia.

And then as a red dawn streaked the sky, the guests began to take their leave. One by one the carriages began to roll out through the tall iron gates. One by one the guests who were too drunk to walk were carried out. Many of the local people set out for Trewent village on foot.

The feeling of menace that Yvonne had felt in the hall earlier returned, and she was glad the castle was full of guests.

She said good night to the viscount, longing to ask for another kiss, hoping he would escort her to her room, but he only smiled down at her and told her he would wait to supervise the servants who were clearing away the tables and chairs from the marquees.

But he had said he did not believe she took the diamonds, and he had said they must get to know each other better. If only he had not pulled away so roughly from her kiss.

She went into her bedroom and walked across and pulled back the curtains and opened the window. Yawning, she raised her hands to the heavy tiara and removed it from her head.

"I am so tired," she said aloud.

"Then you are going to feel even more tired by the time I have finished with you, Yvonne de la Falaise," said a mocking voice behind her.

Yvonne swung round.

In the hectic red light of dawn flooding the room, Yvonne saw Patricia Cottingham sitting in a chair.

In her hand she held Yvonne's pistol.

And it was pointed straight at Yvonne's heart.

Chapter Ten

"Sit down," said Patricia. "We are going to wait here quietly until I am sure I can get you from this room unobserved. Take off the jewels, and leave them on the toilet table."

"I was right," said Yvonne. "It *was* you all along."

"Do as you are told," snapped Patricia.

Yvonne placed the diamonds on the toilet table and then sat down on the edge of her bed. She felt sick and cold. Patricia must be mad.

As if replying to that unspoken thought, Patricia said, "No, I am not mad. You may stay alive if you behave yourself. I want you out of the way for a little, that is all."

"Why?"

Patricia looked at her with contempt but did not reply.

Pieces of the puzzle fell into place in Yvonne's mind. The boat below the castle, the old man at the Kennel who thought he had seen a ghost, the new hard, implacable look on Patricia's face.

"You," said Yvonne, "are not Patricia

Cottingham. You are Ellen Tremayne, Black Jack's granddaughter."

"Too clever, too late," the governess said, sneering.

"And the fire and the kidnapping — you arranged those?"

She nodded.

"And how do I address you now, my good governess? As Ellen Tremayne?"

"I am Patricia Cottingham. I changed my name legally."

"You have accomplices," said Yvonne. "I should have thought of that. The door to my bedchamber was locked the night of the fire. Someone disturbed the servants by shouting 'fire' from the other end of the corridor, and when they were gone, he or she unlocked the door to my room. It could not have been you, for at that moment you were demonstrating to Lord Anselm how brave you were in rescuing his ward."

Again, Patricia nodded.

"But who were those brigands in the boat? Local people? Your people from the Kennel?"

"No," said Patricia. "All *they* are fit for is scavenging on the beach. Did you not recognize your own race? They were French."

"French! But I did not understand what they were saying."

"They are Bretons."

I must keep her talking, thought Yvonne. "What have you to do with the French — you, who claim they are an excitable and untrustworthy race?"

Patricia looked amused. "I may as well satisfy your curiosity." She glanced at a watch pinned to her bosom. "We have time." She had changed out of her ball gown into a serviceable cotton gown with a high neck and long, tight sleeves.

"I am indeed Ellen Tremayne. I was brought up in the Kennel. My mother was believed to have been drowned searching for a chest of gold in a wrecked merchantman. But she did not drown. She found it and brought it home. I was hiding behind the door when she showed it to my father. He said the money should be used to turn me into a lady, to get me away from the Kennel. My mother jeered at him and said the gold had to be shared among their accomplices. He struck her a heavy blow — too heavy. She was killed outright. So he carried her out into the bay and threw her body into the sea.

"I was six years old at the time. We escaped to France after the funeral. The hostilities with England had not yet recommenced, and we were able to go about freely. He settled in Brittany and put me into a convent. At the age of sixteen, he took me out and forced me to marry an elderly French gentleman, a bourgeois. His name does not matter. He did not live long."

She gave a mirthless laugh, and Yvonne wondered whether her husband had been allowed to die a natural death.

"I asked my father for my share of the gold. He had lost it over the years, gambling in every filthy hovel and den. My husband had left all of his money to his relatives. So I was a lady, an educated lady, but as poor as I had been in the Kennel.

"My father died of an apoplexy not long after the death of my husband. I took another husband to save myself from starvation. People who did not know my background considered I had married beneath me. He was a fisherman, and I soon found out he was smuggling spies, information, and wine over to England.

"I convinced him I could be a great help to them were I allowed to reside on the English side. That way I could warn them of the movements of the excisemen. I quickly found out about the old dungeons below Trewent Castle. Wine, goods, people, and papers could be stored there. We could come and go at night. I found them an island, several miles off this coast, that they could use as a base.

"My fisherman husband was killed in a drunken brawl, and I took over his organization.

"When I read the viscount's advertisement in the local paper, I saw my chance. My convent education had not taught me much, but I felt sure I could pass muster. How much better to run things from inside the castle itself.

"Life became easier when I arranged for two English accomplices to obtain posts as footmen in the castle almost immediately after my arrival."

She fell silent and tilted her head a little to one side, listening to the diminishing sounds of bustle coming from outside as one by one the servants finished their duties and went to bed.

"But you started after juicier game," said Yvonne. "You saw a chance of becoming Lady Anselm."

"And I would have succeeded," said Patricia, her eyes blazing with fury, "had you not gone out of your way to stop me. Well, you shall pay dearly for your folly."

"How? In what way?" demanded Yvonne through dry lips.

"I am taking you over to France, where you will be held prisoner until I have secured the affections of Lord Anselm."

"But why should you want him? Why?"

"He is rich, I admit. But I love him, love him as a silly virgin like you could not even begin to understand."

Her anger subsided as quickly as it had risen, leaving her as cold as ice. The pistol in her hand did not waver.

Keep her talking, thought Yvonne. I must keep her talking.

"The men in that boat who kidnapped me," she said. "They were in disguise. I have a feeling they were very young."

166

"They are little more than boys. The young ones are the loyal ones. The older ones, because I am a woman, try to take over from me."

"I went to the Kennel," said Yvonne. "An old man there said he had seen your ghost. But if you left when you were a child, how did he recognize you?"

Patricia shrugged. "The eyes of the old can discern the child in the grown woman. He talked, and it made the people of the Kennel run for hiding. I went back twice to remind myself what might await me if my courage faltered."

"It was you at the window that evening," said Yvonne. "You looked in at the window and saw him put the diamonds on me."

"That was one of my accomplices, one of the footmen. I was sure he must be mistaken. I told him it was impossible to see clearly through the leaded panes. But he said that one of them was clear, and by putting his eye to it, he saw Lord Anselm put the tiara on your head. I knew then I had little hope. I knew even then that you must be removed. And yet I hoped . . . But you, with your sluttish ways, entrapped him that night in Truro. I saw you both at his bedroom window."

"That *was* you I saw." Yvonne sighed. "But you are wrong. I was only in his bedchamber because I thought I saw you in the courtyard of the inn with two men. I ran to his room."

"Could you not leave well enough alone?"

demanded Patricia. "But I can still have him — without you around."

"How do you plan to get out of the castle without being seen?" asked Yvonne. "There is always someone about."

"They will all soon be asleep."

"But someone among the servants must have suspected something," said Yvonne desperately. "*I* saw the boat below the castle."

Patricia gave a short laugh. "When anyone got too curious I had my accomplices frighten them with tales of the ghost of Black Jack. They are very superstitious."

All at once Yvonne realized how quiet the castle had become.

"Yes." Patricia smiled, reading her thoughts. "The time has come."

She stood up. "You will walk in front of me. Remember, should we meet anyone, you will smile and nod. One look of warning, one sound from you, and I will blow your brains out."

Yvonne rose slowly from the bed. "Are you leaving the diamonds?" she asked. "I would have thought a felon such as you would want to take them."

"I shall have them, legitimately, when I am Lady Anselm. Now, move!"

As she passed the toilet table, Yvonne brushed it lightly with her fingers and they closed on a small pair of nail scissors.

Not much of a weapon, but perhaps it could be put to some use.

As Patricia urged her out of the bedroom, Yvonne held the scissors down at her side and snipped at the red and gold fringe of her robe.

Patricia thrust the cold barrel of the pistol against Yvonne's back.

"To the dining room," she whispered. "*Our* dining room, where we have spent so many *cozy* evenings together."

Numbly, Yvonne walked along to the dining room at the end of the corridor and pushed open the door.

"Go over to the wainscoting," she said, closing the door gently behind them, "and press that carved knob to the left of the fire-place."

Yvonne did as she was bidden and gasped in terror as a panel slid back, exposing a flight of stone steps leading downward.

Her last hope of escape had gone. There was no way now that she could meet some servant or wandering guest and try to get help.

Stumbling a little with fatigue and fright, she went on through the panel. There was a click as Patricia closed it behind them, leaving them in total darkness.

With the hard muzzle of the gun against her back, Yvonne groped her way down and down.

"How did you find this staircase?" she asked.

"Someone in the Kennel in the old days had the original plans of the castle, dating from the days when it was a lazar house. They were going to try to reach my grandfather before he

169

was hanged. But the guards lied about the day of the hanging and hanged him a week earlier than anyone expected. But we kept the plans."

After Yvonne felt she had been groping her way downward for an eternity, she came up against a wooden wall.

Patricia leaned over her shoulder and pressed a catch. "Go through and stand still and don't move."

Patricia reached past her and opened a door. The passage came out at the back of a dusty closet. The closet door opened to face the cellar door.

"It is locked, but no matter," said Patricia, taking a key from her pocket.

The well-oiled door swung open silently.

Two figures detached themselves from the shadows of the cellar and walked forward to meet them. With a sinking heart Yvonne recognized two of the footmen — Abel and Jeb. She looked pleadingly at them. They were so very young, surely very little older than she was herself.

But their eyes were shining with hero worship and excitement as they held up a lantern and looked at their leader — Ellen Tremayne, or Patricia Cottingham, as she was now called.

"I suppose you plan to take me down to the old dungeons and from there by boat to France," said Yvonne.

"Very clever of you." Patricia sneered. "You did not think we were going to walk you out of the main door of the castle!"

If, thought Yvonne with a surge of hope, they planned to take her out from the castle by boat, then perhaps someone might see them. She snipped busily away at yet another piece of fringe. The footman called Jeb raised the lantern higher and looked at her. Yvonne hoped he would not look down at the floor, where shreds of red and gold fringe laid a trail from the door of the cellar.

"We'll take her out the usual way," said Patricia.

"She knows the usual way," said Jeb.

"What?"

"I was hiding in the hall last night and heard them talking, her and his lordship. She was telling him how she rung that fire bell when she thought he was going to propose marriage to you and stumbled over the secret entrance."

Naked hate blazed in Patricia's eyes, and she struck Yvonne across her face. Yvonne fell to the floor but leaped up almost immediately and darted to where the black rope of the fire bell hung down.

But before she could reach it, Abel seized her in a cruel grip and swung her around to face Patricia.

"Little fool," hissed Patricia. "One more move like that and I shall shoot you dead. Since you know where the secret door is, go there."

"I have forgotten," said Yvonne, looking wildly around.

171

Patricia nodded to Abel, who urged Yvonne forward, still holding her in a tight grip.

"She knows where it is now," said Patricia. "Release her."

Yvonne stood looking down at the small canvas-covered door.

"It'll be a long time 'fore she can kiss his lordship again." Jeb laughed.

There was an awful silence for a few moments, and then she heard Patricia's voice, high and strained, demanding, "What do you mean?"

"Last night in the hall," said Jeb, "they was hugging and kissing fit to beat the band."

There was another silence. Yvonne turned around. Patricia was looking straight ahead, her eyes completely blank.

Then she said in a quiet, controlled voice, "Go through, Yvonne. I am right behind you."

Yvonne turned around and soon felt the hard point of the gun being driven into her back again.

She got down on her hands and knees and began to crawl through.

"Stand still on the other side," shouted Patricia. "Remember — you cannot escape."

Yvonne stood cautiously upright at the top of the stairs on the other side. She could hear the thud and pound of the sea far below.

Then, all at once, Patricia's voice came right behind her and Patricia's venomous voice hissed in her ear, "Good-bye, you little slut!"

Patricia pushed with all her might and Yvonne went flying.

Had Yvonne been prepared for the attack, then she might have gone rigid, might have tried to save herself, and broken every bone in her body tumbling down the stone staircase.

But as it was, she was so shocked that she took off from the top of the stairs like a bird, sailing out into the blackness. Before she could collect her wits, before she quite knew what had happened, she came to land with a sickening thump.

A roaring world of sea and spray and terror whirled about her eyes and then she lost consciousness.

At the top of the stairs, Patricia called to her two henchmen. "Come through here and bring that lantern."

She moved down the stairs a little to leave room, and then, when the two men had crawled through, she said, "Hold that lantern high. I want to make sure that's the end of her."

Jeb gasped. "You shouldn't ha' killed her. You said we was to wait till nightfall and get the others to take her off to France."

"Less trouble this way," said Patricia with seeming indifference.

"But there'll be a great search when she's found missing."

"Her body will be washed out to sea," said Patricia, "and the next tide will bring it in down the coast. Hold that lantern up."

But the feeble light of the lantern only illuminated halfway down the shattered steps.

"I cannot risk going down there," said Patricia. "Nor can you. She told Anselm about this secret way, and he may by some ill chance be already looking for her. There is no way she could have survived such a fall. In any case, the tide is coming in."

The two men, white to the lips, backed through the hole and into the cellar.

"You've never done that afore," whispered Abel. "You've never killed anyone."

Patricia looked at him coldly.

"She was so very beautiful," said Jeb in an awed voice.

"Oh, I admit she was fair to look on," said Patricia. Her eyes suddenly filled with tears. "Why do you stare at me so? Do you think it was easy for me? Do you think it was easy for me being brought up in the Kennel? I was six when I left there, but I am determined never to return to that level of filth and ignorance and poverty."

"We thought they did well, them wreckers," mumbled Abel.

"They never wrecked anything worth wrecking," said Patricia, "until my mother did it for them. If they did get anything, they squandered it or brought the militia down on our heads. When I was five, I saw ten men — *ten* — from the Kennel kicking out their lives on a gibbet."

She took a deep breath. "Let us get out of

here. I am weary. I have a part to play when the tide washes her body up on the beach."

With drooping shoulders, she led the way out of the cellar.

The viscount strolled about the lawns, watching as the last marquee was brought to the ground.

His mind was full of thoughts of Yvonne. Could he dare hope she might love him — love him as a woman should love a man, and not as a girl forms a *tendre* for an older man?

Patricia must be sent away. That was another thought that troubled him. He had a guilty conscience. He had, at the beginning, treated her more familiarly than he should have treated any governess, however gently bred. And, yes, he had encouraged her to believe he might propose marriage.

But surely his behavior toward her in the past weeks should have driven any such ambitions from her head. He had been correct and formal every time he had spoken to her. But he still cursed himself for his own folly.

His mind swung back to Yvonne. He had no right to propose marriage to her while she was still so young. She must see something of London society first.

It was only when he had been sending invitations out to the ball that he had realized what a dearth of eligible men there was in the county.

He would send Yvonne to London for the

Little Season. He racked his brains trying to think of a suitable household where she might live and a suitable chaperone to bring her out.

He became aware that Fairbairn was at his elbow and was trying to get his attention.

"It's the diamonds," said the butler reproachfully. "Apart from the ones that my lady was wearing to the ball, they are on the table in the morning room in full view."

"What a fool I am!" said the viscount. "Listen, Fairbairn, I allowed my ward to wear the jewels because I became convinced she did not take them. But if she did not take them, then someone else most certainly did. I should never have left them lying around. Come with me and we shall find another safe place for them."

Fairbairn followed his master to the morning room. After some thought, the viscount decided it best to put the jewels with his own jewels in the strongbox in his bedchamber.

"And when I have done that," he said, "I had better recover the others from my ward."

When he walked along to Yvonne's bedchamber, he vowed he would not wake her, although the temptation to speak to her again and to study the expression in her eyes was very strong.

He scratched at the door of her room.

No reply.

After some hesitation, he pushed open the door and went in.

Sunlight winked on the tiara and necklace on the toilet table.

But Yvonne's bed was unslept in, and of Yvonne there was no sign.

He seemed to hear Gustave's voice in his head telling him that one day he might find he had lost something more precious than the Anselm diamonds.

He crossed to the window and opened it and looked out. The rising wind streamed into the room. Black clouds were beginning to cover the sun, and the sea had turned a greenish-black color — a sure sign of a coming storm.

Sharp, irrational fear gripped him. The sound of the waves pounding at the base of the cliffs was greedy and evil.

He tried to tell himself she had gone off on one of her mad expeditions. But all of the strange things that had happened to her crowded into his mind.

He went next door to Patricia's room and opened the door. She lay fast asleep. There were the marks of recently shed tears on her cheeks, and once again he felt guilty, feeling obscurely he must have been the cause of her distress.

He turned about and went downstairs, calling for his servants, rousing them from their sleep, demanding his ward must be found.

Then he went to the stables to look for Gustave.

With any luck, he might find Yvonne in Gustave's room.

But Gustave, struggling from sleep, immediately looked worried and alarmed when he heard Yvonne was missing.

Bursting into voluble French, he insisted the governess be awakened and questioned. He, Gustave, had thought long and seriously about his mistress's suspicions of Miss Cottingham. He felt they had not taken Yvonne seriously enough.

But guilt over his own behavior toward the governess made the viscount insist the castle and grounds be searched first.

The wind was rising, and thunderheads piled up in the sky. The viscount quickly changed out of his evening dress into a shirt and breeches and, taking Gustave with him, mounted the stairs to Patricia's bedchamber.

This time Patricia awoke as they entered. Her eyes moved from the viscount's worried face to the hard, suspicious stare of Gustave, who was standing behind him.

"Where is my ward?" demanded the viscount.

"I do not know," said Patricia, sleepily struggling up against the pillows.

"Her bed has not been slept in."

"Then she has probably gone out riding."

"Her horse is in the stables."

"Walking, then. You know how she is. . . ."

Gustave gave a snort of impatience and went out and along to Yvonne's bedchamber, hoping to find something the viscount might have missed. Perhaps she had left a note.

He crossed the room and closed the window against the rising gale. The diamonds blazed and sparkled from the toilet table with a light of their own.

Gustave felt a stab of dread. Yvonne would have never disappeared, carelessly leaving such jewels unprotected.

He was about to leave and go back to join the viscount when little shreds of gold and red fringe lying on the floor of the bedroom caught his eye.

He bent down and picked some of them up. They seemed to have been cut off rather than torn off.

He saw they formed a sort of trail out into the passage. The little shreds lay here and there along the passage in the direction of the dining room.

His heart beating hard, he went to get the viscount, some inner voice preventing him from blurting out his discovery until he had led the viscount outside the governess's bedchamber.

Outside in the passage, Gustave put a finger to his lips and pointed at the floor. Together, they followed the trail left by Yvonne until they found it mysteriously ended against the wall of the dining room.

"There must be a secret way," muttered the viscount. "It will take all day to find it. Get me an axe."

"No! The pieces of material stop right here,"

said Gustave. "Let me try."

He felt along the carving on the paneled wainscoting, pushing and pressing until his fingers encountered the knob.

Both men stood back as a panel in the wall slid open.

"Get a lamp from Yvonne's room," said the viscount, his face grim.

Gustave went back out into the passage and along to Yvonne's room.

Patricia was waiting at the door to her bedchamber. "What is it?" she cried. "Have you found her?"

"Go back inside your room," shouted Gustave. His eyes blazed with suspicion and dislike, and Patricia backed away before them.

Gustave seized an oil lamp and returned to join the viscount.

They lit the lamp and, with Gustave carrying it and the viscount leading the way, they followed the mysterious stair down and down.

Near the bottom, the viscount stopped with an exclamation. "Yvonne told me of a secret entrance in the cellars," he said. "Let us go straight there."

"But the little bits of material are still here," said Gustave, "marking the way she must have gone. 'Tis best we follow them."

On they went again until they emerged from the closet by breaking through it — the viscount was in no mood to waste precious time searching for hidden catches — and found themselves opposite the cellar door. Patricia had forgotten to lock it behind her.

The viscount darted into the cellar, looking desperately this way and that, and Gustave, holding the lamp and bending double, followed the little bits of fringe, but they ended in the middle of the floor.

"She found this entrance when she was down here, ringing the fire bell," said the viscount. "Bring the lamp over to where the rope is."

In his haste and anxiety, he tore barrels away from the walls and sent them rolling into the middle of the cellar.

"Ah," he said with a note of satisfaction. "I have it. Come here, Gustave."

There was the painted canvas, and there on the floor in front of it one little thread of red fringe.

The viscount knelt down on the floor and pushed his way through into the blackness on the other side. From below came the thudding and pounding of the sea.

"The lamp, Gustave," he called over his shoulder. "Come through, man. She must be here somewhere!"

Yvonne's fall had been from the top of the stairs to the bottom. Had she hit the stairs themselves, then her neck would have been broken. But various tides washing into the old dungeons had formed a sort of sandy beach at the foot of the staircase. As it was, she plummeted down on this beach, and although she had been knocked unconscious by the sheer force of the impact, she had not broken any bones.

The first wave of the incoming tide struck her on the face, and she stirred slowly and opened her eyes.

All about her on the sand lay huge chunks of masonry. There had been a floor above that had been eroded by the winter tides and had fallen in.

On jutting pieces of the old floor above, she could make out the dim shape of barrels in the light filtering in from the mouth of the cave. The cave entrance was actually a breach in the old dungeon walls made when the level of the sea had risen.

Another wave struck her. Realization of the peril in which she lay caused her to struggle feebly and try to sit up. But her body was racked with pain, and she felt sick and dizzy.

She collapsed again and lay with her cheek against the sand, tears of weakness from her eyes trickling down to mingle with the salt water of the sea.

Then she gasped as a huge wave poured over her and started to drag her back.

Panic lending her strength, she began to painfully crawl on her hands and knees toward the staircase.

The tide was rising fast.

The air was full of the wash and thud and

clamor of the water.

The wind outside had risen, and it shrieked and moaned above the noise of the water. Yvonne closed her eyes, thinking she was hearing the screams of the condemned. They would have been chained to the walls in the room that used to lie above, hanging in their chains, night after night, listening to the wild, free surge of the tides.

She clawed her way up the first few stairs, but a huge wave crashed over her, plucking her from the staircase and dragging her back like some huge monster dragging its prey back to its lair.

She clutched onto a broken piece of masonry until the wave subsided.

"Anselm!" cried Yvonne piteously. "God help me. God have mercy and give me the strength to escape."

She raised her eyes and thought she saw a sign from heaven.

A golden light was descending the staircase, a golden glow far above her head.

With a tremendous effort, she crawled forward again, scrabbling up the stairs, sobbing for breath.

But a giant wave like some watery demon's hand plucked her body from the steps, and with a despairing cry, Yvonne de la Falaise disappeared in a tumult of black and green water.

Saltwater filled her mouth and roared in her ears. She had no strength left. She could feel the next wave picking her up and knew she would be dashed against the broken, jagged foot of the staircase.

And then she felt strong arms close about her. She heard a beloved voice cry, "Yvonne!" and then she lost consciousness again.

Carrying her limp, inert body, the viscount struggled out of the water.

"Up," he said to Gustave. "Go ahead with the lamp and light the way. Then ring the fire bell. Summon everyone."

Patricia sat huddled in a chair in her room. Gustave had looked at her as if he *knew.*

Getting rid of Yvonne had been so simple. Just one push. Patricia had intended to take her to France. But when she had heard of the viscount and Yvonne embracing, she had decided on the spur of the moment to kill her. She shivered, imagining Yvonne's body being tossed and tumbled by the sea.

Never before had she been troubled with religious thoughts. Now she began to fear for her immortal soul.

"If You did not want me to do it, God," she muttered, "then why did You bring me up in violence and poverty?"

And then the fire bell began to ring.

She put her hands over her ears to block out the sound.

The viscount must be ringing for help.

She must be brave. She must go down with

the others and join in in their surprised exclamations and questions.

Patricia scrambled into her clothes and went out into the passageway. The whole castle seemed to reel under the deafening sound of the bell.

She looked along in the direction of the dining room and stiffened.

The door to the dining room lay open, and she distinctly remembered having closed it behind them.

Like a sleepwalker she went along to the dining room, stifling a scream when she saw the secret panel lying open.

It was then that she looked at the floor and saw the trail of scraps of bright silk fringe.

She took a deep breath to steady her nerves. It would appear as if Yvonne had gone exploring and had found the secret passage.

If she kept her head, then nothing could be proved against her.

She squared her shoulders and walked out of the dining room, back along the corridor, and began to descend the stairs. Sleepy and alarmed guests were tumbling out of their bedchambers.

The violent clamor of the bell ceased. Down below in the hall there came the rise and fall of voices, like the rise and fall of the sea.

She walked down to the first landing.

And stopped.

All of the staff were assembled in the hall.

White faces stared up at her.

Mounting the staircase with Yvonne cradled against his chest came the viscount. And behind him came Gustave, his eyes shining with a red light of rage when he saw the governess.

For Yvonne had recovered consciousness in the cellar for one brief moment, and in that brief moment she had murmured, "It was Patricia. She is Black Jack's granddaughter," before passing out again.

Gustave made a leap for the stairs, and Patricia turned and fled.

Up and up she ran with the whole household, headed by Gustave, at her heels.

She ran to the top of the castle and mounted the ladder that led up through a skylight onto the roof.

The day was black and stormy. Wind tore at her skirts and sent her golden hair flying about her head.

She stood at the edge of the battlements overlooking the sea and watched as Gustave's grizzled head and broad shoulders rose above the skylight.

He looked at her and said clearly and distinctly in English, "Do not worry. You shall not live to hang. For I am going to break your neck."

He advanced on her with clutching hands.

Patricia whirled about and dived clear from the top of the battlements.

Gustave dashed to the edge and looked over.

Had the wind not been so very stormy and very violent, Patricia might well have dived clear into the sea and, being a powerful swimmer, might have managed to escape.

But a great gust of wind snatched at her, as the incoming waves had snatched at Yvonne's body, and hurled her down onto the stone flags of the terrace below.

Gustave felt the other servants crowding behind him.

"Do not look," he said, turning around to face them. "It is not a pretty sight."

Patricia's two accomplices, Abel and Jeb, were found hiding on the moors. A whole army of constables, soldiers, magistrates, and excisemen descended on the castle during the following days to examine the old dungeons and take away evidence of smuggling and spying from the remains of the old cells. A naval party rounded up the Breton smugglers from their island off the coast.

Yvonne, weak and ill, answered questions as best she could.

Jeb and Abel might have escaped, for Yvonne did not recover consciousness until the day after her rescue, when she was able to give the authorities their names.

The viscount could barely bring himself to leave her side.

He slept on a chair beside her bed, watching anxiously and waiting, talking to her in a soothing voice when she started up with one of her many nightmares.

He was tortured by a bad conscience. How could he have been so stupid, so blind, as to view a murderess with complacency, thinking her a paragon of all the virtues and even at one point contemplating proposing marriage to her?

He was now more than ever determined that Yvonne should go to London when she had recovered. There she might meet some man worthy of her.

She looked little more than a child, lying asleep with her hand on her cheek and her black hair tumbled on the pillow.

The physicians had recommended a change of scene for Yvonne when she recovered. It was important, they said, to remove her for a while from Trewent Castle and its memories.

Stormy days passed, one after the other, as summer fled before the gales of autumn.

Color returned to Yvonne's cheeks and brightness to her eyes.

She and the viscount talked at length about Patricia — Patricia, who was really Ellen Tremayne, the pirate's granddaughter.

At last, Yvonne was able to get up and go out.

She lived for each moment she saw her guardian and happiness enhanced her beauty.

But gradually she became aware that although her guardian treated her with loving tenderness, it was the love of someone toward a delicate child and not the love of a man for a grown woman.

Her near escape from death and her subsequent illness had removed much of Yvonne's confidence. She felt she could no longer tease him or ask him to kiss her.

And so when her guardian finally went off to London and returned a month later to say he had made arrangements for her to be chaperoned by a certain Lady Baillie, Yvonne brightly thanked him and said she was very excited at the proposed visit to the metropolis.

And the viscount thought he had finally learned his lesson when it came to dealing with the fair sex and did not even guess that his little ward spent her last night at Trewent Castle in tears.

Chapter Eleven

London, with its social glitter, its noise, its fashions, parties, routs, and scandals, swirled around Yvonne.

Lady Baillie was a distant connection of Lord Anselm. She was a widow, tall, autocratic, and frigid of manner. But she knew where her duty lay. Yvonne de la Falaise was to be presented to as many members of society as were still to be found in town.

She was hardly a suitable companion for a young girl, but the viscount had wanted his ward guarded by a dragon.

Yvonne had come to assume in the easygoing atmosphere of the country that English misses were blessed with a great deal of freedom.

In London she found the opposite. The scandalous free and easy days of the last century, when women rode astride to hounds and even attended assemblies in men's clothes, had gone. The rising middle class, although still banned from the temples of the haut ton, had made their mark.

Strict morality was the order of the day, *before*

marriage. It appeared no one cared much what one did after marriage.

Had not Lady Caroline Lamb startled her husband's guests by allowing herself to be served up for dinner in a huge silver-covered dish? When the cover had been removed, there she had been, stark naked, without even an orange in her mouth.

But she was still to be seen gracing Almack's, the holy of holies where assemblies were held on Wednesday evenings and a virgin could be cast out of its august doors for tying her garter in public.

Virginity was worshipped as never before, and a debutante must do *nothing* to make it appear she had lost it, or her value on the Marriage Mart would plummet. And among the things she must not do were laugh too loudly or boldly, wear too much rouge, cross her legs in public, and sit down on a chair whose seat was still warm from some gentleman's bottom.

Lady Baillie lived in South Molton Street in a bleak, well-run house. She never entered into a companionable conversation with Yvonne, merely confining any remarks to instruction as to which events to attend and how to go on when one got there. She also shouted very loudly at Yvonne when she did speak, being under the impression that all foreigners were stone deaf.

The days were dark and cold. One woke in darkness and went out for the evening in darkness. Only occasionally was a small pale sun, like a burnt-out planet, to be seen dimly through the fog that blanketed the winter city.

After much deep thought and private anguish, Yvonne decided her guardian did not love her in the slightest. This sending her to London was his way of fulfilling his obligations without having to take on any of the responsibilities himself. When they had conversed in Yvonne's bedroom during her illness, the viscount had often talked with regret about Patricia, saying it was a vast pity that such a seemingly capable and sensible female should prove a villain, and Yvonne, who did not know of the viscount's guilt regarding Patricia, could only assume he heartily wished she had never been found out so that she might continue to take the chaperonage of his ward off his shoulders.

For a time, Yvonne was depressed and barely noticed any of the gentlemen who paid court to her. Lady Baillie was pleasantly surprised and wrote to Lord Anselm to say that his ward was a very prettily behaved young miss.

Gustave, much to the viscount's surprise, had been ordered by Yvonne to remain behind at Trewent Castle. But Gustave knew why. He, Gustave, was to act as spy on his lordship's activities and state of mind and send bulletins to his mistress.

His letters, laboriously penned in shocking English — Gustave was receiving lessons from

Mrs. Pardoe — did little to cheer Yvonne. His lordship, he wrote, appeared well and in good spirits and was getting about a bit and had even attended a ball at a country house near Exeter.

Yvonne eventually replied with a cross and angry letter saying she had come to the conclusion that her guardian had no interest in her.

Shrewd Gustave thought about that for a long time and then replied there had been no report from Lady Baillie to cause his lordship any concern. He often asked his lordship what the news was from London, and his lordship always replied that Lady de la Falaise was the soul of decorum.

Yvonne studied Gustave's letter. Hope that had died in the winter fogs and in the parsimonious cold of Lady Baillie's establishment began to glimmer again.

What would the viscount do if he *were* made to worry about her? Why, he would come to London to see for himself!

She had used none of her large allowance on clothes, contenting herself by dressing in her Portuguese ensembles.

All at once, the startled Lady Baillie began to notice her charge was indulging in an orgy of fashion. The house was full from morning to night with dressmakers, mantuamakers, and milliners.

Then came the evening of the Hartcourts' ball. Lord and Lady Hartcourt were accounted among the most tonnish of the ton, and the cream of society crowded into the gilded rooms of their Grosvenor Square mansion.

Lady Baillie saw Yvonne's outfit for the first time in the glare of the chandeliers when Yvonne appeared in the ballroom, having left her cloak downstairs.

She was wearing one of the new gauze over-dresses. Her slip of an underdress was of the finest muslin and clung to her body in a way that left little to the imagination. Her hair, which heretofore had been severely braided, fell about her shoulders in wanton glossy black curls.

She not only flirted with the eligible men; she flirted outrageously with all of the ineligible men as well. Feeling faint, Lady Baillie counted three adventurers, two rakes, and one card-sharp in Yvonne's circle of courtiers.

Lady Baillie gave Yvonne a terrible tongue-lashing after the ball. As Yvonne shivered on the hearth rug before a glimmer of a fire, Lady Baillie ranted and raved, talking about the re-duction in her market value as if she were a commodity on the stock exchange.

Yvonne sweetly promised to behave herself, with such a penitent mien and downcast eyes that Lady Baillie was confident that never again would her charge behave so dreadfully.

The following evening at the Italian opera, Yvonne was demurely and fashionably dressed. Once more, her neckline was modest and her hair braided. Like Almack's, the Italian opera was confined to the Exclusives, apart from the prostitutes in Fops Alley and the servants in the gallery.

Lady Baillie, as was her practice at the opera, fell asleep five minutes after the curtain arose.

Wild cheers and shrieks from the audience awoke her from a peaceful slumber, and she gazed at the stage in horror.

Yvonne, who must have managed to climb down to the stage from the sidebox, was happily engaged in singing a duet with the tenor.

Her voice was quite good and very sweet, but the enraged prima donna bounded onto the stage and tried to scratch Yvonne's eyes out. Yvonne tripped her up, and she fell headlong, where she pounded the stage with her fists and went into strong hysterics.

The bucks in the pit roared their approval of Yvonne and started to throw oranges and rotten vegetables at the prima donna. Law officers were called in to try to quell the ensuing riot, but the evening was wrecked. As was the custom in theater riots, the harp was the first thing to be smashed, followed by the piano-forte.

Women screamed and fainted. Two men in the boxes started a sword fight. The prostitutes were openly displaying their wares in a quite disgusting way. Someone took out a pistol and tried to shoot out the flames of the candles in the great central chandelier that hung from the ceiling.

Then someone shouted, "Fire!" and that was the end of the elegant evening at the opera as everyone pushed and shoved to get out.

Lady Baillie was beside herself with rage, a rage that was heightened to apoplexy point when she found that Yvonne had made her escape through the stage door as soon as the riot had started and was calmly waiting for her in South Molton Street.

"I shall write to your guardian — *express*," said Lady Baillie awfully.

This statement made Yvonne bear all the subsequent lectures and social disgrace with equanimity. Surely he would come *now*.

But Yvonne had not made allowances for Lady Baillie's great pride.

They were sitting in silence at the breakfast table some four days later when Lady Baillie broke the silence by saying abruptly, "I have decided to give you one more chance. I have not written to Anselm of your disgraceful behavior. He would consider me incompetent, lacking in authority. We shall go on as if nothing has happened."

"Thank you, my lady," said Yvonne quietly. She left the room and ran upstairs to her bedchamber and cursed and swore.

After a time, she began to feel calmer. Perhaps all was not lost. The newspapers, of which there were fourteen dailies, had all covered her scandalous behavior in their columns. She lifted out the pile of press cuttings she had saved, put them in a package, and sent them to Gustave with a note telling him to be sure to show the contents to Lord Anselm.

The viscount was sitting in the library, studying more plans for the modernization of Trewent Castle, when Fairbairn entered and said that Gustave wished to see him.

"Very well," said the viscount. "Show him in."

He had often wondered why Yvonne had allowed her faithful servant to stay behind. When he went out riding, Gustave often trotted behind him on his placid mount, unasked, saying only that he felt like the exercise. It appeared to the viscount and his staff as if Gustave had transferred all his crusty affection from Yvonne to the master of Trewent Castle — for none of them knew of the bulletins Gustave sent to London, not even Mrs. Pardoe, who often taught the French servant English and entertained him with glasses of blackberry wine in her parlor.

Gustave strode into the room, a sheaf of cuttings from the newspapers in his hands.

"Milord!" he blurted out. "We must leave for London immediately."

"What is wrong?" asked the viscount, standing up, as visions of marauding Bretons sailing up the Thames to murder Yvonne flashed through his mind.

Wordlessly, Gustave held out the pieces of newspaper.

The viscount took them, sat down, and raised his quizzing glass to study them, for the lamps had not yet been lit and the light in the library was poor.

Gustave waited impatiently while the viscount read them all with maddening slowness.

"Has she lost her wits?" said the viscount, turning a horrified face up to the old servant. "Singing on the stage like some common trollop. Why did Lady Baillie not let me know of this?"

"Perhaps," ventured Gustave, "this Lady Baillie has not got a strong enough hand to control milady.

"Milady can be very wild and reckless at times," he added, noticing with satisfaction the angry flush of color on the viscount's face.

"Tell the servants to prepare my traveling carriage," snapped the viscount. "We leave for London immediately."

"I shall go, too," said Gustave. It was a statement, not a question.

All during that long journey to London, Lord Anselm fretted and fumed. Throughout the long dreary weeks of Yvonne's absence, he had carried a tender picture of her in his mind, a picture of Yvonne as she had been when she was ill, delicate, and childlike, and in need of cherishing.

But her shocking behavior brought back a picture of that other maddening Yvonne, who flirted with her large black eyes and encouraged him to kiss her.

She was probably flirting with every rake in London. She had behaved like a courtesan, and society would treat her like a courtesan.

Snow was beginning to fall, and the lamplighter was making his rounds as the viscount's muddied traveling carriage rolled to a stop outside Lady Baillie's house in South Molton Street.

Tired as he was, he could not bear to sit formally in the carriage while his footman sounded the knocker, but jumped down and thundered on the door himself.

Lady Baillie's butler, Perkins, was a timid man with an unfortunate stammer — Lady Baillie had hired him at cut rate from an agency — and it seemed to take him hours to choke out that Lady Baillie and Lady de la Falaise had gone to a musicale at the Bentleys' mansion in Berkeley Square.

"Then bustle about and show me to a room where I may change," snapped Lord Anselm. "Gustave, help the servants unload my imperials and send my valet to me immediately."

The nervous butler showed him into a bleak bedchamber dominated by a large antique four-poster bed. The air of the room was stale and cold.

"Why is there no fire?" said the viscount. "Oh, never mind," he added hurriedly as the butler was winding himself up for a long speech. "Have one lit as soon as possible and bring hot water, lots of it."

He did not know the Bentleys, but with all the arrogance of a good-looking man of rank and fashion with a considerable fortune, he was sure of his welcome.

At last, attired in black coat and black silk knee breeches, with his bicorne under his arm and his hair teased into the Windswept, he set out to walk to Berkeley Square, which was only a short distance away.

"How on earth," he raged to himself as he walked along Brook Street and turned into Davies Street, "could Lady Baillie be so stupid as to take her around society after her disgrace?"

The Bentleys lived at Number 19. A butler answered the door and, after surveying his jewels and his dress, stepped aside to let him past, murmuring that the musicale was in progress in the ballroom.

A German tenor was singing Mozart arias to a bored audience.

Heads turned as he entered the room and then quizzing glasses were raised.

"I declare," said an elderly matron next to Yvonne, "that devilishly handsome fellow Anselm is back in London."

Yvonne's heart began to beat hard. She longed to turn her head and look at him but was afraid of the love and longing that would show on her face.

Lady Baillie had been wise to take Yvonne

around in society. So prim had Yvonne been since that night at the opera, so correct in her behavior, that the scandal of her theatrical appearance had begun to be replaced by juicier scandals and she was in danger of being castigated as a missish bore. Only the stern patronesses of Almack's still eyed her with disfavor and vowed to turn down her application should she prove impertinent enough to ask for vouchers to their assembly rooms.

The viscount's eyes raked the room. Then, at the very front of the audience, he saw the top of Yvonne's neatly braided head.

He waited impatiently. The concert seemed to go on forever. Light snow was still falling, and outside the windows the plane trees, planted in Berkeley Square at the time of the French Revolution, raised slim whitened branches to the black sky.

The concert finished with an excruciating series of ballads, sung by a fat lady with asthma, dressed as a shepherdess.

Then the guests were told to go through to the supper room.

The viscount waited at the door for Yvonne and Lady Baillie.

But there were so many people he knew, so many hopeful ladies fluttered about him, that he nearly missed them and just succeeded in breaking away from his adoring audience in time to catch Yvonne by the arm and swing her around to face him.

Although Yvonne had expected his anger, she had foolishly dreamed that the very sight of her might cause him to melt into tenderness. The reality was very different from the dream. He was glaring at her as if he wanted to wring her neck.

Blue eyes met black in a long, hard stare.

"And just what do you think you have been playing at?" snapped the viscount. "Making a fool of yourself at the opera?"

"You are making a scene," said Yvonne. "Everyone is looking at us."

He flushed slightly as he became aware of all of the curious eyes and listening ears.

"Anselm," said Lady Baillie nervously. "To what do we owe this surprise visit?"

"I shall discuss it with you afterward," he said. "Now, Yvonne . . ."

But Yvonne had pulled free and had already moved into the supper room, and Lady Baillie saw with a sinking heart that she was already beginning to flirt outrageously.

Yvonne had meant to behave in a contrite manner when she saw him again. After all, she had been prepared for his rage. But the very sight of him overset her. Deep down, she was terrified he might view her with indifference, and his rage was preferable to that.

Lady Baillie looked nervously at the viscount. He looked as if he were about to explode.

And then explode he did.

Yvonne was just about to sit down at table. An

adoring cavalier was holding a chair out for her.

Suddenly the viscount descended on her, his eyes blazing and his fists clenched.

"On your feet, young woman," he said. "Come with me."

"No," said Yvonne. "I am very hungry, and I am about to have supper."

He let out a roar of rage. As the guests scattered, he snatched her up bodily, threw her over his shoulder, and strode for the door.

"Oh, the scandal, Anselm!" wailed Lady Baillie.

Yvonne screamed and pummeled his back with her fists, but he walked straight out of the mansion, only setting her down when he reached the bottom of Hay Hill.

"Bully!" raged Yvonne. "I shall catch the ague."

"Now," he said, holding her by the shoulders and glaring down at her, "you will tell me what possessed you to perform on the stage and to begin to flirt like a Cyprian."

She glared back at him, and then, to his amazement, she began to laugh.

"Oh, Anselm," she said with a catch in her voice, "how else could I bring you to London?"

"What?"

"As long as you had reports that I was behaving like a well-mannered miss, you seemed content to forget about me. I could not *bear* that. So I decided to behave badly to bring you to town."

He gave her a little shake.

"Why?" he asked, his eyes burning down into her own.

Yvonne gave a little shrug. Lowering her eyes, she said, "Because I love you."

He put his arms slowly about her and drew her gently to him. He softly kissed her lips and then her cheeks while the snow fell softly all about them.

"Oh, Anselm," murmured Yvonne, "is that the best you can do?" She wound her arms tightly about his neck and kissed him with all the passion and longing that had been pent up for weeks.

Mr. Tommy Struthers, that well-known Bond Street fribble and pink of the ton, went back into the Bentleys' mansion, brushing snow from his hair.

"Well?" demanded a chorus of voices. "Are they kissing, or is he beating her?"

"Kissing her." Mr. Struthers grinned. "I take the money, I think. Pay up, gentlemen. Trouble is, you fellows don't recognize love when you see it."

"Yvonne," said the viscount finally, freeing his lips. "You are going to marry me."

"Very soon?"

"As soon as possible. Oh, my little love, you are so cold and wet. There are warmer places to embrace."

He led her in the direction of South Molton Street, stopping every now and then to kiss her breathless.

Gustave stood by the window, watching their passionate progress along South Molton Street as the entwined figures were lit by the feeble light of the parish lamps.

"Dieu soit benît," said Gustave, heaving a sigh of relief. "Now I can get me a good night's sleep."

Once indoors, the viscount augmented Lady Baillie's parsimonious drawing room fire with several shovels of sea coal and sat down with Yvonne on a sofa in front of it, holding her close to his side and dreamily watching the flames.

"Why did you not tell me before?" said Yvonne. "Why did you not tell me you loved me?"

"I was afraid of my own passions," he said. "You are so young, so innocent."

"And have a passion to match yours." Yvonne laughed, drawing his head down.

Half an hour later the butler opened the drawing room door and then retreated hastily in time to witness Lady Baillie's flustered arrival.

"Good evening, Perkins," said Lady Baillie. "Is Lord Anselm here? I was never more shocked in my life. I must talk to him."

She put her hand on the handle of the drawing room door.

"No!" cried Perkins. "You m-must n-not."

205

"Oh, dear," said Lady Baillie, letting her hand fall.

"Oh, yes," said Perkins.

Lady Baillie rallied. She turned instead and headed for the stairs. "A special license, I think," she said firmly. "I don't know what the world is coming to. That is the trouble with this generation. No morals."

Inside the drawing room, the viscount put Yvonne gently from him.

"I never thought it would be I who would have to restrain *you*," he said, grinning.

"Wait for our wedding night, my beautiful ward. Just wait!"

The employees of G.K. Hall hope you have enjoyed this Large Print book. All our Large Print titles are designed for easy reading, and all our books are made to last. Other G.K. Hall Large Print books are available at your library, through selected bookstores, or directly from us.

For information about titles, please call:

(800) 223-1244
(800) 223-6121

To share your comments, please write:

Publisher
G.K. Hall & Co.
295 Kennedy Memorial Drive
Waterville, ME 04901